'You're pregnant!'

'Yes', she said softly. 'With our baby. Maybe you recall an afternoon in August?'

Recall it, he thought raggedly. He would never forget it as long as he lived. The softness of her in his arms again, his mouth on hers, her desire matching his. Hope had been born in him that day.

It was why he was here, in the place where Georgina had made a new life for herself—a life that she was making it clear he wasn't included in. But nothing she said could take away the joy of knowing that those moments of madness were going to bring a new life into the world—their child.

Dear Reader

Having been brought up happily enough in a Lancashire mill town, where fields and trees were sparse on the landscape, I now live in the countryside and find much pleasure in the privilege of doing so. It gives me the opportunity to write about village life with its caring communities and beautiful surroundings.

So, dear reader, welcome to the second of my four stories about Willowmere, a picturesque village tucked away in the Cheshire countryside. During the changing seasons you will meet the folk who live and work there, and share in their lives and loves.

Spring has come to Willowmere when Georgina and Ben meet up again, after a long separation brought about by the kind of heartbreak that either makes a stronger bond between those experiencing it or, as in their case, drives them apart. In A BABY FOR THE VILLAGE DOCTOR, they discover that the flame of love still burns brightly.

Happy reading!

Abigail Gordon

The Willowmere Village Stories
Look out for David and Laurel's story in the summer!

A BABY FOR THE VILLAGE DOCTOR

BY
ABIGAIL GORDON

MILLS & BOON®
Pure reading pleasure™

First published in Great Britain 2009
Harlequin Mills & Boon Limited,
Eton House, 18-24 Paradise Road, Richmond, Surrey TW9 1SR

© Abigail Gordon 2009

ISBN: 978 0 263 20916 7

Set in Times Roman 10½ on 12¼ pt
15-0209-47305

Printed and bound in Great Britain
by CPI Antony Rowe, Chippenham, Wiltshire

Abigail Gordon loves to write about the fascinating combination of medicine and romance from her home in a Cheshire village. She is active in local affairs, and is even called upon to write the script for the annual village pantomime! Her eldest son is a hospital manager, and helps with all her medical research. As part of a close-knit family, she treasures having two of her sons living close by, and the third one not too far away. This also gives her the added pleasure of being able to watch her delightful grandchildren growing up.

Recent titles by the same author:

IN MEMORY OF MY FRIEND
IRENE SWARBRICK RNA SWWJ

CHAPTER ONE

IT WAS a bright spring morning but as Georgina Adams drove along the rough track that led to the gamekeeper's cottage on the Derringham Estate she was oblivious to what was going on around her.

April was just around the corner and daffodils and narcissi were making bright splashes of colour in cottage gardens. Fresh green shoots were appearing in hedgerows and fields where lambs covered in pale wool tottered on straight little legs beside their mothers.

On a normal day she would have been entranced by the sights around her but today the beauty of the countryside in spring wasn't registering.

The only new life that Georgina was aware of was the one she was carrying inside her. She was pregnant and though there was joy in knowing that she was going to have a child, there were clouds in her sky.

Ben had never replied to the letter she'd sent, explaining that they needed to talk, and that she would travel to London to see him if he would let her know when it would be convenient. The weeks were going by and he didn't know about the baby.

She'd only written the once, and it had been very difficult, agonising over what to say and how to say it, because she wanted to tell him that he was going to be a father again face to face. He was entitled to know that he'd made her pregnant, and she needed to be there to see his reaction.

In the end she'd written just a few bald sentences, sealed the envelope before she changed her mind, and gone straight away to post it to an address that she knew as well as she knew her own name. He hadn't replied, and it was now beginning to look as if that was the end of it.

The fact that the baby's father didn't know she was pregnant was the biggest cloud in her sky, but the hurt and loss from over three years ago had never gone away. Remembering how Ben had been then, it wasn't altogether surprising that he hadn't been in touch, but she did wish he had.

Half of the time she was gearing herself up for the role of single parent and for the rest she was battling with the longing to have Ben beside her as she awaited the birth of their second child.

At almost eight months pregnant there was no way of concealing it and she was conscious all the time of the curious stares of those she came into contact with. She'd lived alone since she'd joined the village medical practice three years ago as its only woman doctor and had kept her private life strictly under wraps.

To her colleagues at the practice, her patients and the friends she'd made since settling in the Cheshire village of Willowmere, Georgina was pleasant and caring, but that was as far as it went.

The only person locally who knew anything about what was going on in her life was James Bartlett, who was in charge of village health care and lived next door to the surgery with his two children.

He had told her that if she ever needed a friend, she could rely on him, and had left it at that. James hadn't asked who the father of her baby was, but she knew he would have seen her around the village with Nicholas during the weeks leading up to Christmas and it would have registered that he'd not been on the scene since the New Year.

Soon she and James would have to discuss her future role in the practice, but before that happened, replacements were required for two staff members who had recently gone to work in Africa.

When she stopped the car outside the grace-and-favour cottage of the woman she'd come to visit, the husband came striding out, dressed in a waterproof jacket with boots on his feet, a cap on his head and to complete the outfit he had a gun tucked under his arm.

Dennis Quarmby was gamekeeper for Lord Derringham, who owned Kestrel Court, the biggest residence in the area, and with it miles of the surrounding countryside. But at that moment the main concern of the man approaching was not grouse or pheasants, or those who came to poach them on his employer's estate.

His wife was far from well and on seeing that the lady doctor from the practice had arrived in answer to an urgent request, he waited for her to get out of the car before going on his way.

'Our eldest girl is with the missus,' he told her, his anxiety revealed in his expression. 'I wanted to be here when you came but Lord Derringham has just been on the phone to me because someone has been breaking down the fences up on the estate and he wants me there right away. He rang off before I could tell him I was waiting for a doctor to visit Christine. Her eyes and mouth are so dry she's in real distress, and with the rheumatoid arthritis, as well, she's feeling very low.'

Georgina nodded. She'd seen Christine Quarmby a few times recently and on one occasion had had to tell her that she was suffering from rheumatoid arthritis. Now there was this and there could be a connection that had serious implications.

When she went inside the cottage, the gamekeeper's wife said, 'Has my husband been telling you my tale of woe, Doctor? He does worry about me, though I have to admit I'm struggling at the moment. I'm having trouble swallowing, as well as everything else that is wrong with me.'

It was clear that the glands that produce tears and saliva weren't working, Georgina thought, in keeping with some sort of autoimmune disorder. But it required the opinion of a neurologist before she prescribed any medication and she told Christine, 'I'm going to make you an appointment to see a neurologist and the rheumatologist that you saw when we were trying to sort out the rheumatoid arthritis. We'll see what they come up with.'

'I know someone who has the lupus thing,' Christine said. 'You don't think it's that, do you, Doctor?'

'I wouldn't like to make a guess at this stage,' she told her, surprised that her patient had been thinking along the same lines. 'I'll ask for an urgent appointment and we'll take it from there.'

As she was leaving, Dennis returned and announced that as soon as he'd informed his employer that his wife was ill, he'd told him to forget the fences and come home.

'Christine will tell you what we've discussed, Mr Quarmby,' Georgina told him, 'and in the meantime send for me again if she gets any worse.'

'I'll do that, all right,' he promised. 'She plays everything down, having been made to suffer in silence when there was anything wrong with her when she was a kid, and thinks she shouldn't complain, which is not the case when there's anything wrong with me. I do that much moaning, everybody knows.'

'Yes, well, look after her. She needs some tender loving care,' she told him. 'I'm sending Christine to see two of the consultants at St Gabriel's and hopefully we'll have a clearer picture of what is wrong when she's been seen by them.'

When she returned to the practice in the main street of the village, it felt strange, as it had done for days with Anna and Glenn no longer there. Anna Bartlett was James's sister and had been one of the practice nurses.

On a snowy day in January she had married Glenn Hamilton, who'd been working at the surgery as a temporary locum, and in early March the newlyweds had gone to Africa to work with one of the aid programmes out there, before returning to Willowmere to settle down permanently.

They needed to be replaced and soon, or she and James would be overwhelmed by the demand for their services, and though she intended working until the baby was due, she would need time off afterwards. So some new faces were going to be needed around the surgery without delay.

It was lunchtime and James was having a quick bite when she appeared. 'The kettle has just boiled,' he told her. 'How did you find Christine Quarmby?'

Her expression was grave. 'Not too good, I'm afraid. There is something very worrying about her symptoms. Christine thinks she might have lupus, which as we know has connections with rheumatoid arthritis, and she could be right, though I do hope not. I'm referring her back to the rheumatologist she saw before and am going to arrange for her to see a neurologist, as well.'

'Hmm, there isn't much else you *can* do at this point,' he agreed. 'By the way, Georgina, I'm interviewing this evening for another doctor and a practice nurse. Beth Jackson is struggling single-handed in the nurses' room, and we haven't yet had anyone come in as another partner since the gap that was left when my father died.

'I would have liked Glenn to become permanent. He was an excellent doctor, like yourself, but it didn't work out that way. Do you want to sit in on the interviews, or will you have had enough by the end of afternoon surgery?'

'I'll give it a miss, if you don't mind,' she told him,

'unless you especially want me to be there.' She gave a wry smile, 'I'll be the next one to cause staffing problems, but not until after the baby is born.'

'Don't you worry about that,' he said. 'Just take care of yourself, Georgina. With regard to the interviews, I'll bring you up to date with what's gone on in the morning, so go and put your feet up when the surgery closes. It's only a fortnight to Easter. Why don't you go away for a few days?'

'I'll think about it,' she promised, and made a pot of tea to have with the sandwich she'd bought at the bakery across the road.

'How many applicants have you had for the two vacancies?' she questioned as he prepared to go back to his duties.

'There have been quite a few. I've sifted out the ones that sounded suitable and once the children are asleep, I'll be coming back for the interviews. Their daytime nanny finishes at half past six, which coincides with the end of my time here under normal circumstances, but Helen, my housekeeper, has offered to be there for Pollyanna and Jolyon tonight.'

When Georgina let herself into the cottage on a quiet lane at the far end of the village, it still felt empty without the lively presence of Nicholas. It had been nice to have her ex-husband's brother around for a while.

He'd been based in the United States since just after she and Ben had divorced. The offer of a job in aerodynamics that he'd long coveted had come up and he'd been torn between taking it and staying to help them sort out their lives. Both of them had insisted that *his* future mattered more than theirs and he'd gone, though reluctantly.

Nick had been back a few times and stayed with them both alternately. He'd done the same this last time when he'd come over to Manchester to arrange the U.K. side of the firm that employed him in Texas, staying with her during the week and spending his weekends with his brother in London as part of a situation where she and Ben never made any contact.

If she had ever felt the necessity to get in touch, as was now the case, Georgina knew where Ben could be found. It was she who had moved out of the house in a leafy London square all that time ago. A house where, in that other life, the two of them had lived blissfully with Jamie, their six-year-old son.

Jamie. It had been losing him that had taken the backbone out of their marriage and, like other loving parents before them, tragedy hadn't brought them closer, it had driven them apart.

She knew that Nicholas hated the situation he found himself in with the two people he cared for most in the world, yet he wasn't a go-between. Georgina had made him promise that he would never divulge her whereabouts to Ben without her permission. Even though she knew Ben was the last person who would come looking for her after all they had been through.

As she made a meal of sorts, Georgina was remembering how Nicholas had taken her to Willowmere's Mistletoe Ball in the marquee on the school sports ground, and he'd gone with her to the gathering at James's house on Christmas Eve when Anna and Glenn had announced their engagement. So she supposed the senior partner at the practice could be forgiven if he had Nicholas down as the father of her baby.

It had been August when something she'd not been prepared for had happened. She'd been at Jamie's graveside, taking the wrapping off the white roses that she always brought with her, when a voice had said from behind, 'Hello, Georgina.'

She'd turned slowly and he'd been there, Ben Allardyce, her ex-husband, the father of the cherished child they'd lost.

He'd looked older, greying at the temples, and the emptiness that had never left his eyes after Jamie had been taken from them had still been there in the gaze meeting hers. As she'd faced him, like a criminal caught in the act, she'd known that no other man would ever hold her heart as Ben had.

Nicholas had told her that Ben knew she visited the grave, but during all the time they'd been apart she'd never come across him until that day which had also been Jamie's birthday.

She'd turned back to the labour of love that had brought her there and was arranging the flowers with careful hands on the white marble of their memorial to their son.

When it was done and she'd straightened up and faced him again, he'd said, 'Nicholas tells me he's coming to the U.K. in October and is going to be here three months. It will be good to see something of him.'

'Yes, it will,' she answered awkwardly, like a schoolgirl in front of the head teacher.

'Do you want to come back to the house for a drink before you drive back to wherever you've come from?' he asked in the same flat tone as when he'd greeted her. She observed him warily. 'It was just a thought,' he explained, and she wanted to weep because of the great divide that separated them.

'Yes, all right,' she heard a voice say, and couldn't believe it was hers. She turned back to the grave once more and dropped a kiss on the headstone, as she always did when leaving, and when she lifted her head, he was striding towards his car.

'You know the way, of course,' he said as she approached her own vehicle. She nodded, and without further comment from either of them they drove to the house that had once been their family home.

As she stepped inside, the sadness of what it had become hit her like a sledgehammer. The room began to spin and he caught her in his arms as she slumped towards him.

She rallied almost as soon as he'd reached out for her, but Ben didn't relax his hold. They were so close she felt his breath on her face as he said, 'You need to rest a while.' Picking her up in his arms, he carried her to the sofa in the sitting room and laid her on it.

When she tried to raise herself into a sitting position he told her, 'Stay where you are. I'll make some tea. A brandy would be the ideal thing but as you're driving…'

After he'd gone into the kitchen she looked around her and saw that nothing had changed in the place that had once been her home. Furniture, carpets, ornaments were all the same as she'd left them, and she thought numbly that it was them who had changed, Ben and herself, heartbreakingly and irrevocably.

Jamie had been taken from them in a tragic accident, and with his going their ways of grieving had not been the same. Hers had taken the form of a great sadness that she'd borne in silence, while Ben had been filled with anger at what he saw as the injustice of it, and it had turned him into someone she didn't recognise.

Instead of comforting each other, they had become suffering strangers and in the end, unable to bear it any longer, she'd asked for a divorce. Still fighting his despair, he'd agreed.

He'd offered her the house but she'd said no as it wasn't a home to her any more. She'd packed her bags and gone to take up a position as a GP in a pretty Cheshire village that was far away from the horror of those months after Jamie had drowned.

When Ben came back with the tea he put the cup and saucer down and, with his arm around her shoulders, bent to raise her upright. 'I never expected to see you actually here in the house again when I set off for the cemetery.'

'Neither did I,' she murmured, and as she looked up at him their gazes met and held, mirroring sadness, pain, confusion…and something else.

There was no sense or reason in what happened next. He bent and kissed her and after the first amazed moment she kissed him back, and then it became urgent, a tidal wave of emotion sweeping them along, and they made love on the sofa on a surreal August afternoon.

When it was over, he watched without speaking as she flung on her clothes, and when she rushed out of the house and into her car, he made no attempt to follow her.

It wasn't until after Nicholas had come to stay that Georgina had realised she was pregnant. She'd been feeling off colour for a while, nauseous and light-headed, but busy as ever at the practice hadn't thought much of missing her monthly cycle as she had always been irregular, initially putting it down to stress.

All the signs had been there—tender breasts, tired-ness, morning sickness—and she'd faced up to it with a mixture of dawning wonder and dismay while care-fully concealing it from her house guest. It hadn't been too difficult as, although she'd been five months along by the time he'd returned to America in the New Year, she'd barely shown at the time. Even James hadn't re-alised until she'd told him. Now, however, at eight months, her bump was there for all to see.

Knowing Nicholas, he would have felt he had to tell Ben if he'd found out about the baby, she'd thought, and she'd needed time to adjust to the situation that had come upon her so suddenly. Every time she thought about the wild, senseless passion that they'd given in to on that August afternoon, she wanted to weep. They'd lost a child born in love and gentleness. Under what circumstances had this one been conceived—loneliness, opportunism?

As the weeks had passed, the knowledge that she wasn't being fair to Ben had pressed down on her like a leaden weight until the night she'd written the letter. After that she'd felt better, and had begun the ritual of watching out for the postman every morning, but there'd been no reply.

She could have called him. It might have been easier. But she was afraid that she might give herself away on the phone, and she just *had* to tell him face to face. No matter how they'd parted after losing Jamie.

It had been Jamie's attachment to his football that had sent him careering over the edge of the riverbank. The ball had started to roll down the slope where she'd parked the car for the two of them to have a picnic.

She'd turned away to lift a folding chair out of the boot, and as she'd been erecting it had seen him, oblivious to danger and ignoring her warning to keep away from the edge, running towards the swollen river.

It had all happened in a matter of seconds and as she'd flung herself down the slope after him and shrieked for him to stop, he hadn't heard her above the noise of the fast-flowing water.

She'd nearly lost her life trying to save their son and when she'd been dragged half-dead from the river to discover that she was going to have to carry on living without him, she'd wished that she'd died, too.

Ben gazed at the letter in his hand. Each time Nicholas had visited since that August afternoon, he had asked him where he could find Georgina, but he'd reluctantly refused to tell, explaining that she'd made him promise never to pass on that information.

It hadn't been hard to believe when Ben recalled how she'd never come near the house apart from that one time when he'd found her at Jamie's grave. Whenever he'd seen fresh white roses on it he'd known that she'd been just a stone's throw away from the home they'd shared together, and the despair that had become more of a dull ache than the raw wound it had been during those first awful months would wash over him.

He'd thought bleakly that what had happened between them on the day he'd caught her unawares in the cemetery hadn't seemed to have made Georgina relent at all, and if Nicholas wasn't prepared to break his word to her, it was going to be stalemate.

On his last night in London his young brother had asked, 'Why are you so keen to find Georgina afer all this time?' And because there had been no way he was going to tell him what had happened, Ben had fobbed him off by telling him that some insurance in both their names had matured.

That had been in early January, and when Nicholas had flown back home Ben had gone to work in Scandinavia for a short while. He'd always been somewhat of a workaholic, even before their marriage had broken up, getting a lot of satisfaction out of helping sick children and being able to give Georgina and Jamie some of the good things in life at the same time.

When their life together had foundered after losing their son he'd immersed himself in his work more and more, and had spent less and less time at home. Without Jamie it wasn't a home any more.

When Georgina had asked for a divorce he'd agreed, because he'd felt their life together was over. They'd had no comfort to offer each other—he, because of the terrible bitterness inside him, and she because she felt responsible for what had happened.

But that day in August he'd discovered that their feelings weren't dead. There was still a spark there. It had been sweet anguish making love to the only woman he'd ever wanted, and he wasn't going to rest until he saw her again.

He'd gone to Scandinavia with less than his usual enthusiasm, because he was frustrated and miserable to think that she'd come back into his life and given him hope and then disappeared into the unknown once more.

Now he was home again, and amongst the mail that had accumulated during his absence was the envelope with Georgina's handwriting on it. With heartbeat quickening, he opened the letter.

The brief communication inside said that she needed to talk to him as soon as possible, and it went on to say that she would come to London if he wished. No way, he thought. He'd waited a long time to find out where she'd gone, and now the opportunity was here.

She hadn't used the word urgent, but there was something about the wording of the letter that conveyed it to him, and as the postmark on it was from weeks ago he immediately began planning how quickly he could get to this Willowmere place in Cheshire.

Ben was freelance, and not attached to any particular hospital, so there were no arrangements to make at his end. After a quick snack, and a phone call to arrange overnight accommodation at a place in Willowmere called the Pheasant, he was ready for the off, warning the landlord that he would be arriving in the early hours.

As she did on most evenings when she'd eaten, Georgina set off for a short stroll beside the river. A heron, king of the birdlife, familiar to all the village folk, was perched motionless on its favourite stone in the middle of the water when she got there, and she remembered how when she'd first moved to Willowmere she'd had to steel herself to look at the Goyt as it skipped along its stony bed.

As the last rays of the sun turned the skyline to gold she felt the child inside her move and wondered if it was going to be a son to follow the one they'd lost or a baby girl with the same dark hair and eyes as her parents.

She knew that under normal circumstances Ben would be over the moon at the thought of another child, but *normal* would have been as a brother or sister for Jamie and he was no longer with them.

They'd created a new life in those moments of wild abandon and it should be a source of joy for them both, but as it stood now *he* knew nothing about it.

She saw that the lights were on in the surgery as she walked back to the cottage and brought her thoughts back to the situation there. Would James find suitable replacements tonight for Anna and Glenn?

After a bath and a hot drink, she was tucked up in bed half an hour later and thinking drowsily that for half the population the night would only just be beginning, but tomorrow would be another busy day for her and James.

She awoke in the early hours to the noise of a car pulling up on the quiet lane below, but didn't get up to investigate. Instead she snuggled lower under the bed-covers with her eyes closed. The doors were locked, the burglar alarm on. Whoever it might be, she was too sleepy to check them out.

As he'd driven through the Cheshire countryside, Ben had thought wryly that Georgina had certainly intended to put some distance between them by coming here, and she'd also chosen a beautiful place to come to.

He'd seen a lake glinting through trees in the light of a full moon as he'd approached the village, and as he'd drawn nearer had seen that the main street was made up of cottages built from limestone next to quaint shops that made the present-day supermarket seem an uninteresting place by comparison.

He'd arrived earlier than expected, and had stopped briefly outside Georgina's cottage on a lane at the end of the village after receiving directions from an elderly man.

The curtains were drawn, for which he'd been thankful, as it was hardly the hour to be calling. After choking back the overwhelming feeling of regret for all the wasted years they'd spent, he'd driven off into the night to find his accommodation.

Knowing as he did so that ever since he'd found

Georgina in the cemetery and persuaded her to go back to the house, then made love to her like some madman, he'd been aching to see her again. Desperate to tell her how he regretted the way he'd behaved when they'd lost Jamie.

He'd been like someone demented and had vented his desolation on to her, as if she hadn't been suffering, too. If he'd been in charge, the tragedy would never have happened, he'd told her at times when he'd been at his lowest ebb, and it had been as if the love they'd shared had also died.

It hadn't been until in bitter despair she'd asked for a divorce and left because she'd been unable to stand it any more that he'd faced up to what he'd done to her.

He'd given her the divorce, couldn't for shame not to after the way he'd behaved, and ever since then had longed to have her back in his life. He wanted to tell her how sorry he was for forsaking her when she'd needed him, for being so selfishly wrapped up in his own grief without a thought for hers, and to explain how meeting her that day had brought all his longing to the surface in an enormous wave of passion.

There'd always been amazing sexual chemistry between them, but after losing Jamie they'd never made love, so estranged had they become. Now he was going to try to rebuild the marriage that had crumbled, and maybe Georgina wanting to talk was a step in the right direction.

CHAPTER TWO

WHEN Georgina looked through the window the next morning, there was no car to be seen so she concluded it must have driven off after stopping for a moment.

After a shower and a nourishing breakfast she was ready to leave, and with the car already outside from the previous day, she was about to slide into the driver's seat when she looked up and saw a man walking towards her along the deserted lane.

He was tall and dark-haired with a trim physique. As he approached she stared at him in disbelief and when he stopped at the bottom of her drive and said, 'Hello, Georgina,' in the same tone of voice as on that day in August, her legs turned to jelly.

'So did you get my letter?' she croaked from behind the car door.

'Yes, but only a few hours ago,' he said evenly. 'It had been lying unopened behind my door for weeks. I've been abroad recently. So what's the problem, Georgina? What do you want to talk to me about?'

So far the car door was concealing her pregnancy but

she couldn't stay behind it for ever, and with a sudden desire to shatter his calm she pushed it shut. Looking down at her spreading waistline, she said, 'I want to talk to you about this.'

It was Ben's turn to be dumbfounded. 'You're pregnant!' he gasped. 'Oh! My God! You're with someone else! Why didn't Nick tell me?'

'Nicholas didn't tell you because there was nothing to tell,' she informed him steadily. 'He doesn't know I'm pregnant, and as for the rest, there is no one else in my life. I am on my own and prefer it that way. You are the one who has made me pregnant, Ben. Maybe you recall an afternoon in August.'

Recall it? he thought raggedly. He would never forget it as long as he lived, the softness of her in his arms again, his mouth on hers, her desire matching his. Hope had been born in him that day.

It was why he had come to the place where Georgina had made a new life for herself, hoping that the matter she wanted to discuss was getting back together. Only here she was, carrying his child and making it very clear she hadn't been having any such thoughts. Yet nothing she said could take away the joy of knowing that those moments of madness were going to bring a new life into the world, another child to cherish. It wouldn't ever replace Jamie in his heart, but there would be no shortage of tenderness and love for this one…if he was given the chance.

'What happened that afternoon was the last thing I intended,' she told him as they faced each other on the drive. 'Nothing was further from my mind, and now I'm carrying the result of what we did.'

'And you aren't happy about it?'

'Yes, of course I am. I'm happy that I'm going to have another child. It is a privilege I never anticipated, but after losing Jamie and the dreadful aftermath, I'm not intending to change my lifestyle as it is now, except for doing fewer hours at the practice maybe.'

'Fair enough,' he said evenly, stepping to one side as she slid behind the wheel. 'And is this baby that you've been keeping to yourself going to get to know its father as it grows up?'

'If our lives had been as they were before we lost Jamie, it would have been ecstasy to tell you that I was pregnant,' she said sadly. 'Because our child would have been conceived in love, like he was. But it wasn't like that, was it? Too much water has flowed under the bridge since the days when we lived for each other and him.'

'But you *were* prepared to tell me that you're pregnant, Georgina, though in your own time. I suppose it could have been worse. I could have arrived to find you pushing a pram. And so is my part in this going to be sitting on the fence?'

'No, of course not,' she said, choking on the words. 'It's just that I couldn't go through what I suffered before if anything should happen to this child. I understood your despair but you never tried to understand mine. You shut me out, Ben, and it broke my spirit. Since I've come to Willowmere I've found a degree of comfort in the place and its people, but no one knows my past and that is how I would prefer it to stay.'

'So you don't want anyone to know that we were once husband and wife?'

'I'm not bothered about that, and in any case it's a problem that won't arise as you won't be around.'

'Don't be too sure about that,' he said dryly. 'I'm my own boss these days, and am due for a break anyway.'

Ignoring his comment and its implications, she expained, 'It's the reason for the divorce that I don't want to be common knowledge. I don't want anything to spoil Jamie's memory.'

'You can rest assured that I, of all people, won't be telling anyone why we broke up,' he said grimly. 'But, Georgina, I feel you need to know that if I had any intention of my stay here being brief, it won't be now. I'm going to be around until the birth *and after*, so please take note of that.'

He was stepping away from the car and, as she began to drive slowly out onto the road, he called through the open window, 'When I've settled my account at the pub I'm going home to tie up all the loose ends and then I'll be back. I'm not sure when, but I *will* be coming back.'

She had no reply to that. Still numb with the shock of seeing him strolling towards her along the lane, she left him standing at her gate.

As she pulled up outside the surgery, Georgina's thoughts were in chaos. There was relief that Ben now knew about the baby, tied up with panic at the thought of him coming to Willowmere and invading the solitary, safe life she had made for herself. Beneath it all there was

a glimmer of happiness, because in spite of the circumstances, she'd given him something to be joyful about.

She did wish he'd let her know he was coming, though,
so she could have greeted him with calmness in her sitting
room, dressed in something that would have concealed
her pregnancy during the first few moments of meeting,
instead of hovering behind the car door in a state of shock.

Yet her surprise had been nothing compared to his
when he'd realised she was pregnant, and straight away
jumped to the conclusion that she was in a relationship
with someone else.

James was at the surgery before her but, then, he always was, for the good reason that he lived next door.
After they'd greeted each other, she asked how the
interviews of the evening before had gone, hoping to
bring normality into a very strange morning.

'I've found an excellent replacement for Anna,' he
told her, observing her keenly, 'but there was no one
that I could visualise as a new partner. I feel it might
be wise to leave that until Glenn comes back to
Willowmere. So it looks as if we might be turning to a
locum again for the time being.

'And what about you?' he asked with a smile. 'How
are you today, Georgina? You're very pale. Is the baby
behaving itself?'

She managed a grimace of a smile. Apart from
Beth, the remaining practice nurse, James was the
only one who ever mentioned her pregnancy. Everyone observed a lot, but no one actually said anything
outright and she wondered just how curious the locals
were about her pregnancy.

With regard to herself, she'd been coping just as long as she didn't let her mind travel back to that afternoon in the sitting room of the house where she'd once known such happiness. But that frail cocoon had been torn apart just an hour ago when Ben had appeared and discovered why she'd wanted to talk to him.

James, in his caring way, had noted that she wasn't her usual self and suddenly she knew that she had to tell someone what had happened before she'd arrived at the surgery. She couldn't keep her life under wraps any longer if Ben was going to be around.

'My ex-husband turned up this morning,' she said in a low voice. 'I didn't know which of us was the most dumbfounded, though for different reasons. I had no idea he was coming, and on his part he had no idea I was pregnant.'

'Poor you!' James exclaimed. 'How long is it since you saw him?'

'It had been three years, until we met unexpectedly eight months ago.'

'And you are about eight months pregnant,' he said slowly.

'Yes,' she agreed flatly, 'the baby is his.'

'And what does he think about that?'

'He is delighted.'

'So is that good?'

'It might have been once.'

'I see. Well, Georgina, I don't want to pry into your affairs, but I'm here if you need me. Obviously you have a lot on your mind. Do you want to take the day off?'

She shook her head. 'No, thanks, James. I need to

keep myself occupied. I will remember what you've just said. You are a true friend.' And before she burst into humiliating tears, she went to start another day at the village practice.

'By the way,' he called after her as she went towards her room, 'St Gabriel's have phoned with appointments for Christine Quarmby. The neurologist will see her on Thursday and the rheumatologist the following day.'

She paused. 'That's brilliant. I pulled a few strings and it seems that it worked. I'm very concerned about Christine. I just hope my fears for her aren't realised. On a happier note, have you heard from Anna and Glenn yet?'

'Yes. They've arrived safely and are already working hard.' James filled her in on Anna and Glenn's assignment before she went to her room and called in her first patient of the day, grateful to have her mind taken off the shock of seeing Ben again.

The day progressed along its usual lines, with Beth still managing but relieved to know that a replacement for Anna had been found. The two nurses had been great friends and Anna had been delighted when James had taken on Beth's daughter, Jess, as nanny for his two young children.

The children were fond of Jess. Aware that she was going to be missing from their lives for the first time since they'd been born, Anna had been happy to know before she'd left Willowmere that the arrangement was working satisfactorily.

Georgina's second patient was Edwina Crabtree.

She was one of the bellringers in Willowmere who helped send the bells high in the church tower pealing out across the village on Sunday mornings and at weddings and funerals, but it wasn't her favourite pastime that she'd come to discuss with her doctor

'So what can I do for you, Miss Crabtree?' Georgina asked the smartly dressed campanologist, who always observed her more critically than most when their paths crossed. She had a feeling that Edwina had her catalogued as a loose woman as she was pregnant with no man around, and thought wryly that *loose* was the last word to describe her.

She was tied to the past, to a small fair-haired boy who hadn't seen danger when it had been there, and 'tied' to the man who had been hurting so much at the time that he'd become a stranger instead of a rock to hold on to.

Edwina was in full spate and, putting her own thoughts to one side, Georgina tuned into what she was saying, otherwise the other woman was going to have her labelled incompetent, as well as feckless.

'The side of my neck is bothering me,' she was explaining, 'just below my ear. I didn't take much notice at first but the feeling has been there for quite some time and I decided I ought to have it looked at.'

'Yes, of course,' Georgina told her. After examining her neck carefully and checking eyes, ears and throat, she asked, 'Do you ever get indigestion?'

'All the time,' she replied stiffly, 'but surely it can't be connected with that. I thought you would just give me some antibiotics.'

'Before anything else I want you to have the tests and

we'll take it from there, Miss Crabtree. If you are clear of the stomach infection, it will be a matter of looking elsewhere for the neck problem, but we'll deal with that when we get to it.'

When she'd gone, looking somewhat chastened, Georgina sighed. Oh, for a simple case of lumbago or athlete's foot, she thought. Edwina Crabtree had the symptoms of Helicobacter pylori, bacteria in the stomach that created excess acid and could cause peptic ulcers and swellings like the one in the bellringer's neck.

Christine Quarmby, on the other hand, had all the signs of Sjögren's syndrome, an illness with just as strange a name but far more serious, and she was beginning to wonder what strange ailment she was going to be consulted on next.

Willow Lake, a local beauty spot, was basking in the shafts of a spring sun behind the hedgerows as Georgina drove to her first housecall later in the morning, and she thought how the village, with its peace and tranquillity, had done much to help her find sanity in the mess that her life had become.

As the months had become years she'd expected that one day Nicholas would inform her that Ben had found someone else and it would bring closure once and for all, but she'd been spared that last hurt, and now incredibly he seemed determined to come back into her life. She couldn't help wondering if he would feel the same if she wasn't pregnant.

Robert Ingram owned the biggest of Willowmere's two estate agencies and he had asked for a home visit to his small daughter, Sophie. The request had been received shortly after morning surgery had finished and Georgina was making it her first call.

Apparently Sophie had developed a temperature during the night and a rash was appearing in small red clusters behind her ears, under her armpits and in her mouth.

From her father's description the rash was nothing like the dreaded red blotches of meningitis, but she wasn't wasting any time in getting to the young patient. She never took chances with anyone she was called on to treat, and children least of all.

When Alison, Robert's wife, took her up to the spacious flat above the business Georgina found the little girl to be hot and fretful and the rash that her father had described was beginning to appear in other places besides the ones he'd mentioned.

'It's chickenpox,' she announced when she'd had a close look at the spots. 'Have you had any experience of it before, Mrs Ingram?'

'Yes. I had it when I was young,' Alison replied. 'My mother had me wearing gloves to stop me from scratching when the spots turned to blisters.'

'Good idea,' Georgina agreed, 'or alternatively keep Sophie's nails very short, and dab the rash with calamine lotion. She should be feeling better once they've all come to the surface, and in the meantime give her paracetamol if the raised temperature persists. Has Sophie started school yet?'

'She goes to nursery school twice each week and

is due to start in the main stream in September,' her mother replied.

'We've had a few cases of chickenpox over the last couple of weeks,' Georgina informed her, 'so the infection is with us, it would seem. Sophie should be fine in a few days, but if there is anything at all that you are concerned about, send for me straight away.' She gave a reassuring smile to the anxious mother. 'I'll see myself out.'

When she went downstairs into the shop area she told Robert Ingram, 'I'm afraid that Sophie has got chickenpox, Mr Ingram. The rash is appearing quite quickly and she will feel much better when it is all out. But I've told your wife if either of you have any worries about her, don't hesitate to send for me.'

He nodded. 'Thanks, Doctor. I'm relieved that it is nothing more serious.' And they both knew what had been in his mind.

As she was about to leave, Robert didn't mention that he'd had someone in earlier, arranging to rent the cottage next door to hers for a minimum period of six months. He thought that Georgina would surely feel happier if the other property was occupied, as they were the only two buildings on Partridge Lane.

As he'd watched her drive off that morning Ben had felt shock waves washing over him. How could Georgina have waited so long to tell him that they were going to be parents again? he'd thought dismally. Yet knew the answer even as he asked himself the question.

Georgina had been the butt of his grief and despair when they'd lost Jamie and it would seem she hadn't been prepared to risk a repeat performance by letting him into her life again when they were going to have another child.

He'd felt as if his heart had been cut out when it had happened all that time ago, and if anyone had dared tell him that time was a great healer, he'd turned on them angrily. Now he knew that it was so. The pain was still there, but instead of being raw it was a dull ache and there were actually days when he managed not to think about it.

He didn't know how Georgina had coped over the last three years. When the divorce had come through and she'd disappeared out of his life, the shock of it had brought him to his senses, but not to the extent that he'd done anything about it because he'd been gutted at the way he'd treated her.

Then, unbelievably, they'd met in the cemetery. So what had he done? Without a word of remorse he'd made love to her, and ever since had wanted to tell her all the things he'd never said then.

He'd known that Nicholas knew where she was, that he always stayed with Georgina for part of the time when he was over from the States. Yet until then he'd never tried to persuade him to disclose her whereabouts.

But after that everything had changed, and he'd badgered his young brother for the information with no success.

Now here he was, in the place where she lived, because Georgina had written to him. But if the reception he'd just got was anything to go by, a happy reunion wasn't on the cards.

It was a sombre thought, but it didn't stop him from calling in at the estate agent and making arrangements to rent the cottage next to hers. After he'd collected his things from the Pheasant, he set off on the long drive back to London.

The afternoon seemed endless to Georgina as patients attending the second surgery of the day came and went, and when at last it was time to go, James said, 'I never finished telling you about the new practice nurse. Her name is Gillian Jarvis and she is free to start immediately. I'm expecting her tomorrow morning.

'Her husband has just taken on the position of Lord Derringham's estate manager and like the Quarmbys they'll be living in a grace-and-favour house on the estate. She has a teenage girl at sixth-form college and a younger boy who will attend the village school. The family have moved up north from the Midlands where Gillian was also a practice nurse.

'I'm relieved that is sorted, but we still need someone to replace Glenn either full or part time. However, I suppose we can hang on for a while until the right person comes along,' he said, as he made everywhere secure before they left.

James was aware that she was only half listening and asked, 'Are you going to introduce me to your ex-husband, or will you both still be separate items?'

'Yes and no,' she told him. 'Ben has gone back to London, but he intends to return. I don't know where he's going to stay, and neither do I know how he's going to fill his time. But he told me that with regard to work, he's a free agent, and he needs a break. He also said that he's going to be there for the birth and afterwards.'

And how could she object? It was his child as much as hers. But it wouldn't be like it had been with Jamie. They'd been a family, a happy threesome, wrapped around with love. This time it would be two separate families. Mother and child as one of them, and father with his child the other.

James was observing her sympathetically and she smiled sadly. 'I'm sure you'll meet him soon.'

What she'd said to James was still uppermost in her mind as Georgina took her evening stroll later that day. Her baby *was* going to know its father, as she didn't doubt for a moment that Ben would be back. He'd made that crystal clear. It would be as an older, more sombre version of the husband she'd adored, but a loving father nevertheless.

As she'd told James, she didn't know where he was going to stay. But it couldn't be with her. They might be about to start a new family, but it didn't mean she was going to accept that as a reason for pretending anything that wasn't there.

When she turned to wend her homeward way in the quiet evening the silence was broken by a train en route for the city, travelling across the aqueduct high above the river. Once it had gone there was peace once more down below, and a fisherman engaged in one of the quietest of sporting activities cast his rod over the dancing water.

* * *

It was two days later. Georgina had done some shopping in the village on her way home—meat from the butcher's, fresh bread and vegetables from the baker's and greengrocer's—and as was her custom, she went straight through to the kitchen to start preparing the food.

When she glanced through the window, her eyes widened. Ben was mending a gap in the fence between the two cottages, and as if conscious that he was being watched, he looked up and with hammer in hand gave a casual wave then carried on with what he was doing.

She drew back out of sight and hurried to the front of the house. Surely enough, the 'To Let' sign had been replaced on the cottage next door to one that said 'Let by Robert Ingram'.

Ben had never been in the habit of doing things by halves, she thought as she leaned limply against the doorpost. It was one of the reasons why he was so successful in his career. But this time he'd excelled himself.

Not only had he come to live in her village, but he'd taken up residence almost on her doorstep. Obviously he wasn't intending to miss anything that concerned his pregnant wife and the child she was carrying.

Maybe repairing the gap in the fence was an indication that though he'd sought her out he was going to stay on his own side of the fence, or perhaps on discovering that she was pregnant his interest had moved from mother to child, and until it was born he would be keeping his distance. If either of those things *were* in his mind, shouldn't she be relieved?

Contrary to all the thoughts that had been going through her mind since they'd met at her gate, she went out into the garden and, leaning over the fence, said stiffly, 'I've bought steaks and fresh vegetables and it's just as easy to cook for two as for one. It will be ready in about half an hour if you want to join me.'

He paused in the act of hammering a nail in and looking up, said, 'Er...thanks for the offer, but I've been shopping myself and have a lasagne in the oven.' He hesitated. 'It's big enough for two. It would save you cooking after a busy day at the practice.'

Taken aback by the suggestion, she gazed at him blankly and he groaned inwardly. After the other day's chilly welcome, he had promised himself that now he was established in the village he would take it slowly with Georgina. Keep in the background but be there if he was needed. So what was he doing?

'I only made the suggestion because I've had cause to discover that it's no joke coming home to an empty house and having to start cooking after working all day,' he said into the silence. 'At one time I was keeping the fast-food counters in the stores going, but that didn't last.'

His kitchen door was open. She could smell the food cooking and told herself that Ben asking her to dine with him was no different than her asking him over. They were both doing it out of politeness. It didn't mean anything.

'Yes, all right,' she agreed. 'How long before we eat?'

'Twenty minutes, if that's OK?'

'Yes. It will give me time to shower away the day and change into some comfortable clothes.' Turning, she went back inside with the feeling that she was making a big mistake.

CHAPTER THREE

WHEN Ben opened the door to her twenty minutes later, Georgina stepped into a bare, newly decorated hall that could only be described as stark. When he showed her into the sitting room, it was the same, and a vision of their London house came to mind, spacious, expensively furnished, in the leafy square not far from the park where she'd taken Jamie that day.

Yet Ben was prepared to live in this soulless place and she wondered what was in his mind. He was going to be involved, come what may, but their marriage had foundered long ago. It had hit rock bottom and wasn't going to rise out of the ashes because they'd made a child.

But that occasion had been the forerunner of an unexpected chain of events that had brought him back into her life. Not because he'd known about the baby. That had really rocked him on his feet. He'd come in reply to her letter. Curious, no doubt, to find his ex-wife surfacing from her hidey-hole.

'What?' he asked, observing her expression.

'This place must seem rather basic after our house in London.'

'It's adequate,' he said dryly. 'I long since ceased to notice the delights of that place.' He pointed to a small dining area of the same standard as the rest of the house. 'If you'd like to take a seat, I'll dish out the food.'

This is unreal, Georgina thought as Ben brought in a perfectly cooked lasagne and a bowl of salad, yet she had to admit it was nice to sit down to a meal that was ready to eat after a busy day at the practice.

'So what is there to do in the evenings in this place?' he asked as he served the food.

'Well, you already know the Pheasant in the village, which is the centre of the night life. Everyone congregates there to drink and chat in the evenings. Willowmere is a very friendly place, a small community where everyone cares about everyone else.'

'So you go to the pub every night, then?'

'I didn't say that was what *I* do. My evenings are spent clearing up after my meal and then taking a short walk. This is a beautiful place. I either stroll along the river bank or to Willow Lake, which isn't far away, and contrary to life in the big city, I'm meeting people I know all the time I'm out there, not just because I'm their doctor but because that's what village life is all about.'

She didn't tell him that it had been her lifesaver in the lonely months when she'd first come to live there, when the feeling of no longer being part of the life that she'd once thought would be hers for ever had been unbearable.

'After that I come home, have a hot drink and go to bed,' she concluded.

'So maybe you'll show me around some of these places that you're so fond of,' he said equably, as if not appalled at the similarity of their lives where there was work, lots of it, then coming home to an empty house and a scratch meal, and in his case, watching television for as long as he could stand it before going up to the bed they'd once shared.

'Maybe,' she said noncommittally. 'I suppose you think my life here sounds dull, but it is what I want. I don't ever want another relationship with *anyone*, Ben. Any love I have to spare will be for my baby.'

'Our baby!' he corrected, as his spirits plummeted.

'Yes, indeed. I'm sorry, Ben. It will be *ours*, yours and mine,' she agreed, 'but don't have expectations about anything else.'

'I won't,' he told her steadily, and steered the conversation into other channels. 'You haven't asked me what I'm going to do jobwise while I'm here.'

'No, I haven't, though I have wondered.'

'Don't concern yourself. I'll find something. Do you need any help at the practice or are you fully staffed?'

She gazed at him, open-mouthed. 'We do have a vacancy, but that would be coming down a peg, wouldn't it? I've seen your name mentioned a few times regarding paediatric surgery. You're a high-flyer these days, aren't you?'

'Some people might think so,' he replied dryly, and thought that though he might be good at his job, when it came to coping with grief he'd fallen flat on his face.

'It was just a thought. But if you don't want me around during your working day, just say so. What sort of a position are we talking about?'

'We need another doctor.'

'I see. Interesting. But don't be alarmed, Georgina. I'm not going to crowd you.'

'Not much!'

'You mean my moving in next door?'

'Well, yes.'

'I've rented the place so I will be close at hand if you need me when the baby comes.'

'Right.'

'What? Don't you believe me?'

'Yes, of course I do,' she said. 'I'm sure on some wakeful night on our child's part I will be grateful to have you near, but don't take me too much for granted, Ben.'

He didn't reply. Instead he said, 'Shall we take our coffee into the deluxe sitting room of my new accommodation?'

They spent the rest of the time together talking about the village and when he mentioned the practice again, and the part she played in it, she answered his questions warily.

'This James Bartlett sounds a decent guy,' he remarked. 'I'd like to meet him. Is he married?'

'James lost his wife in a motor accident five years ago, just a few weeks after she'd given birth to twins. Pollyanna and Jolyon are in their first year at the village school.'

'And he's never remarried?'

'No. James and the children live next door to the surgery with an excellent nanny and housekeeper to help out. His sister, Anna, was a nurse in the practice until she married a locum who was with us, and now they've left and gone to work in Africa, leaving James with two replacements to find.

'He's found someone to fill the gap of practice nurse but is hanging fire with the doctor vacancy, saying that he might wait until Glenn Hamilton, his sister's new husband, comes back from Africa to offer him a permanent placing, and in the meantime employ someone on a temporary basis as he did with him originally.'

'It puts more strain on you both, doesn't it, leaving the gap unfilled?' She was getting up to go, feeling they'd talked about the practice enough, and he said, 'You've missed your walk tonight, haven't you? I'm surprised that it takes you by the river. I would have thought it the last place to appeal to you.'

She turned away, thinking that she might have known that Ben would still be out to give her memory a nudge given the chance, and was tempted to tell him that she needed no reminders of what had happened to Jamie and never would.

'A river only becomes a dangerous place because of the elements above and the actions of those of us at its level,' she said in a voice so low he could only just hear it.

If he'd wanted to reply, he didn't get the chance as she was opening the door and telling him, 'Thanks for the meal, Ben.' Then she was gone, out into the spring dusk and back to the place where she'd felt content until now.

Ben watched her go from the window and felt like kicking himself for his apparent insensitivity. He hadn't meant it to be a hurtful comment. It had been said more out of consideration for her feelings, but in the past that hadn't always been the case and he couldn't blame Georgina for freezing up on him.

He'd been congratulating himself that he'd been making progress in getting to know his wife all over again but he'd blown it. Resisting the urge to go after her he turned away from the window, deciding that he'd already been guilty of one moment of bad timing—no point in risking another.

An owl hooted eerily and when Ben turned to look at the clock on the bedside table, it read 2:00 a.m. For most of his life he'd slept with the never-ending sound of London traffic in his ears, but not tonight. Except for the owl, there wasn't a sound out there.

When he raised himself off the pillows and padded across to the window, the moon was shining down on Partridge Lane and he saw the burnished brown of a fox's coat as it slunk along beside the trees on the opposite side.

To a city dweller like himself the rural scene outside his window was strange enough, but stranger still was the thought that next door Georgina was sleeping with their child inside her. Ever since he'd discovered that he was to be a father again he'd been throwing off the mantle of grief that had been heavy on him for so long.

Georgina saying that she wanted no commitments of any kind was something he would have to take in his stride. It was only what he deserved, but he was not going to give in easily. What they'd had before had been very special and he'd cast it and her aside and lived to bitterly regret it.

But now the fates were being kind. He'd found her, and not only was there joy in that, they'd made a child on that August afternoon, and his heart rejoiced every time he thought about it.

Georgina wasn't too happy about the way it had been conceived, but surely she realised that those moments had been more about hunger than lust, a coming together out of the lonely places that they'd found themselves in.

The fox had gone, the owl was silent, and for the first time in years, he was looking forward to what the next day would bring as he went back to bed.

In the cottage next door Georgina was also finding sleep hard to come by. The baby was moving inside her and it was nothing like it had been before when she'd been pregnant.

In those days Ben would have been beside her, sharing in the wonder of the moment by placing his hand gently on the place where the movements were coming from.

Tonight he was nearer than he'd been in years, but still far away in every other respect, and she told the little unborn one, 'Your father is next door and I don't know what to think about that. He didn't know about you until he came, and now he's going to stay. What are we going to do?'

* * *

There was no sign of Ben when she was ready to leave for the surgery the next morning, and Georgina was thankful. She needed a clear head for what she was going to be faced with during the day, and it was more than she'd had the night before.

The shock of his arrival in the new life that she'd made for herself wasn't as acute today and she intended to keep any thoughts of him at the back of her mind until such time as she could view everything more sensibly.

It was another bright spring morning, the kind of day that didn't lend itself to sombre thoughts, and a quick glance at the number of patients waiting to be seen as she passed by to get to her consulting room indicated that the village folk must be feeling the same, as for once, there weren't many.

On being introduced, she found Gillian, the new practice nurse, to be a pleasant, robust-looking woman who seemed to have hit it off with Beth straight away. As James had mentioned, she lived not far from the Quarmbys on the Derringham estate, though in a more prestigious house, her husband being the estate manager, and Georgina was reminded that tomorrow Christine would be keeping the first appointment that she'd made for her at St Gabriel's with her anxious husband by her side.

As she settled behind her desk she could hear the church bells ringing out across the village and thought that Edwina Crabtree's results on the possible stomach infection should be back soon.

The sound of the bells was also a reminder that

though there were the sights and sounds of new life all around, for one family in the village it was going to be remembering a life that was past as they buried an elderly relative that morning in the churchyard not far away.

That same family had just celebrated a birth and old Henry Butterworth's dying wish had been granted when he'd held his new great-granddaughter in his arms the night before he'd passed away peacefully in his sleep.

When she'd gone up to the Butterworths' remote farm on the fringe of the moors to sign the death certificate, Georgina had been met with a mixture of emotions from those there. There'd been delight at the safe arrival of the baby, grief at the passing of the old man, and relief that Henry had been spared further suffering from advanced Parkinson's disease.

As she'd driven back to the surgery on that day a week ago she'd been aware once again of the close family ties of the people in Willowmere. James and Anna had been a prime example of that in the way they'd cared for his motherless children, and Anna would never have left Pollyanna and Jolyon if she hadn't been sure they would be properly cared for by those that James had appointed to take her place.

It made the split between Ben and herself appear a poor example by comparison, but none of those she'd been thinking of had lost a child. *Her* family had ended up as two grieving strangers and how she wished with all her heart that it hadn't been like that.

There'd been no bitterness in her towards Ben. She'd understood his suffering and had felt just great sadness that it had driven her away from him into lonely exile when it should have brought them closer.

Of one thing she was sure, she could not go through that again, no matter how much they loved this new child when it came. But today the sun was shining in a clear blue sky, there was birdsong up in the trees, and as Timothy Lewis seated himself across from her in the middle of the morning, Georgina asked the man who owned Willowmere's secondhand bookshop, 'What can I do for you today, Timothy?'

He was a quiet, unassuming fellow who loved his books. As well as the literary treasures on the shelves of his quaint shop, he prided himself on stocking something for everyone, and whenever she had a moment to spare, Georgina would call in to find a book for bedtime, as sleep wasn't always easy to come by even when she'd had a busy and tiring day.

'I keep having the most awful headaches,' Timothy said in reply to the question. 'A couple of times a month I've been having them and when they come, I can't bear to lift my head off the pillow.'

When she checked his blood pressure, it was only slightly above normal and she asked, 'You haven't had a blow to the head at all?'

'No, nothing like that.'

'Do you feel sick when the headaches come, or have trouble with your vision?'

'Er, yes, both,' he replied. 'I sometimes feel better when I've been sick, and with regard to my eyes I always get flashing lights in front of them as the headache is coming on.'

'It sounds as if you have the symptoms of migraine,' she told him. 'They are easy enough to recognise. What isn't easy in a lot of cases of migraine is to discover what brings it on. Anger, excitement, stress are all factors, and so is diet.' She took some leaflets from a desk drawer and handed them to him. 'These have information on identifying possible triggers and managing the condition. For example, there are some foods that should be avoided, in particular chocolate and dairy foods such as cheese. Also red wine and citrus fruits can trigger it. How long do the headaches last when you get them?'

'It was a few hours at first, but the last time it was a couple of days and I had no choice but to shut the shop, which is my living going down the drain.'

'If they get any worse, come back and see me,' she told him sympathetically. 'In the meantime I can prescribe something to alleviate the pain, and make sure you get plenty of rest. And, Timothy, how about getting someone to help in the shop so that you don't have to close when they occur?'

'I suppose I might have to,' he agreed sombrely, 'but I'm used to my own space. When customers come in, I just leave them to browse. If they want to buy, fair enough, and if not so be it.'

'Come back if the headaches persist or get any worse,' she said as she showed him out. 'And in the meantime try to avoid stress.'

When he'd gone, Elaine, the practice manager, appeared with a message that James wanted a short meeting of staff and would she be free for half an hour first thing next morning before the start of surgery?

Elaine was facing the window and before Georgina could reply, she said, 'Wow! Where has *he* come from? Do you think he's just visiting or has come to live here?'

Georgina swivelled round in her chair and saw Ben strolling along Willowmere's main street in the direction of the shops.

'I know where he's from,' she said flatly as she waved her privacy goodbye. 'And I know why he's here in Willowmere.' Elaine looked at her questioningly. 'His name is Ben Allardyce. He's my ex-husband and he's moved into the cottage next to mine.'

'Really!' Elaine exclaimed, adding in quick contrition, 'I'm sorry, Georgina. I wouldn't have commented if I'd known.'

'It's all right,' Georgina replied. 'You couldn't be expected to know he was connected with me, and if you're wondering about the baby, Elaine, it's his. Ben is the father.'

Elaine was devastated to have been the cause of the reticent dark-haired doctor having to bring her private life into the open, knowing how *she* would feel in similar circumstances, and she said hurriedly, 'What you've just told me won't go any further, Georgina, I promise.'

'I know it won't,' she said wryly, 'but someone will put two and two together sooner or later, knowing village gossip, so there isn't much point in me pretending that Ben has nothing to do with me. Strictly speaking, he hasn't, not now. It's three years since we divorced, but there's nothing to say that *he* won't tell people what the connection is if they see us together. And about the practice meeting, yes, that is fine by me.'

When Elaine had gone back down to her office in the basement with her usual composure missing, Georgina thought that she couldn't imagine the petite blonde ex-accountant, in her late forties and who was the epitome of efficiency, ever having to admit to a failed marriage and an unexplained pregnancy. That, until Ben had come back on the scene, had been her affair and only hers.

She didn't see him come back from where he'd gone. There was too much going on with the patients for there to be time to stand at the window, hoping to catch a glimpse of him to confirm it hadn't been a dream the night before when they'd eaten at the same table in his cheerless rented house.

She wasn't surprised that Elaine had noticed him on the street. He'd always been a man that women took note of, though it had never made any impact on him. He'd only ever wanted her until they'd lost Jamie and then he'd withdrawn into his own grief-filled world and wanted no one.

As she drove home at the end of the day, Georgina was keen to see Ben again. If he'd been in her line of vision at any time during the day, she might have felt differently, but it was almost as if now that he'd entered her world, she had to keep registering his presence to make sure she wasn't imagining it.

She wasn't aware that he'd watched her drive off that morning from the front window of his cottage and had wished that they were going to spend the day together instead of him being left to his own devices, even though he'd known it was a vain hope.

Apart from the fact that Georgina had her commitment to the practice to consider, there was the way she'd reacted on first seeing him. There had been dismay in the dark hazel eyes meeting his, rather than delight, and it had been there again when he'd suggested he might help out at the surgery. But when last had he given her any cause to feel different?

The boot had turned out to be on the other foot. It was *she* who had given *him* joy with the promise of another child to love. After those first few agonised moments when he'd thought it might belong to some other man, he'd never stopped smiling, even though it had cut deep, knowing how long she'd waited to tell him. But that was a bed he'd made for himself and he had no choice but to lie on it.

In the middle of the morning he went into her garden and brought in the line of washing that she'd hung out first thing. On discovering that a fresh breeze had dried it, he fished out an iron and ironing board from one of the cupboards in his kitchen and applied himself to the task.

When the ironing was finished, he decided to go and find some lunch and then do some exploring of the rural paradise where she'd chosen to start a new life. He had passed the surgery with eyes averted and, unaware that he was being observed from one of the windows, had gone to the Pheasant for a ploughman's lunch, before familiarising himself with the delights of Willowmere.

He'd had a change of mind about that while he'd been eating, hoping that Georgina might want to show him around the village herself, which could be an indication that she wasn't as dismayed by his arrival as she was making out. Now he was listening for her car to pull up on the lane that was almost as quiet during the day as it had been during the night.

She was tired, he thought, noting her pallor and the droop of her shoulders as she got out of the car, but when he came out of his door and joined her on the driveway, she straightened up and with a steady smile asked, 'So what has *your* day been like?'

'Different,' he replied, 'and last night even more so.'

'In what way?'

'I saw a fox slinking along by the hedge over there and an owl was hooting somewhere nearby in the kind of silence I'm not used to. It was weird.'

'You weren't impressed, then?'

'Er, yes, I was. Both things were an improvement on the drone of the city traffic, be it night or day. I nearly went to explore the village when I'd had some lunch but thought that you might want to show me around the place yourself.'

'Possibly, but not on a week night. A short stroll by the river or around the lake is my limit, and tonight I have some ironing to do.'

He shook his head and she observed him enquiringly.

'What?'

'It's done. I brought the washing in and ironed it.'

She felt like weeping. It was so long since anyone had done anything for *her*. Instead, she said flatly, 'There was no need for you to do that, Ben. Please don't interfere in my life. I have it sorted. Don't try to change anything.'

'Surely you see that it's already changing with the child that you're carrying,' he said levelly. 'How were you going to manage when the baby came?'

'As I have managed for quite some time. On my own.'

She was tired and wishing she'd never got involved in the conversation that was taking place. It was turning out the way she'd hoped it wouldn't. Ben had been around for only a few hours and he was trying to take charge.

'What about antenatal care? What are you doing about that?'

He was making matters worse and she said stiffly, 'It is sorted. I'm registered privately with a gynaecologist at St Gabriel's. I wasn't going to take any chances with my being on my own. The sense of responsibility is far greater when one is about to become a single parent.'

'It doesn't have to be like that, Georgina,' he said steadily. 'I was the one who made you pregnant, which makes me even more responsible for our baby than you are.'

'Can't we just leave it for now, Ben?' she said dejectedly. 'I'm hungry and tired.' With a vestige of a smile she added, 'Which is not a cue for you to ask if I'm taking any vitamins.'

'Point taken,' he said with a smile of his own, and followed it by suggesting, 'How about I go to fetch some fish and chips? I saw a shop in the village that looked appetising. It would save us both cooking.'

'Yes, all right,' she agreed weakly, aware that it would be the second time they'd eaten together in a situation that was awkward to say the least, but until she'd got to grips with it, that was how it was going to be.

While Ben was gone she showered quickly and changed into a loose pink top and maternity jeans, and had plates warming in the oven and the kettle on the boil by the time he arrived with the food.

When he came inside, he looked around him curiously. This was the place that Georgina had made her home, he thought, when the one they'd made together had been too alien for her to want to stay there.

It was attractive, elegant in a toned-down sort of way, like the woman herself, who was making it clear that she was not going to change anything since he'd appeared on the scene.

With regard to himself he'd drifted into an existence of much work and very little play, but since coming to Willowmere, he was finding a new reason for living in being near his wife again. To him the term *'ex'* didn't apply. Georgina would be his wife until the day he died. He was a one-woman man and since he'd been without her, there had been no others.

'I feel better already,' she told him when they'd finished eating. Regretting the way she'd dealt with his earlier concern, she went on, 'Maybe we could go for the stroll I told you about. Willow Lake isn't far from here and for me that place *is* Willowmere. Needless to say, there are lots of willows there and they really are the most graceful of trees. It is where Glenn asked Anna to be his wife and they were married a month later before going out to Africa on a new and exciting venture.'

'You sound envious.'

The smile was back and this time it wasn't so hard to come by. 'No, not at all. I have lots of things happening in my life at the moment, and, Ben, if you think me cruel for not telling you I was pregnant, there were countless times during the months that have passed when I've started a letter or picked up the phone to tell you about the baby.

'In the end I sat down, wrote to you, and almost ran to the post office. Once the letter was on its way I felt so much better. It never occured to me that you might not be there to receive it. When you didn't get in touch I didn't know what to do.'

'But I found the letter at last, didn't I?' he said gravely. 'And you've given me a new reason for living. What more could I ask?'

It was there again, she thought. The implication that she was going to be the outsider in the forthcoming threesome.

'So shall we go for our stroll, if you really feel up to it, before the light fades?' he suggested, and she nodded. It could have been a special moment, but it hadn't turned out that way.

It was the oddest feeling, walking through the village with Ben by her side, Georgina thought. People going to the Pheasant hailed her as they would normally do, while at the same time casting curious glances at her companion.

Ben said, 'How are you going to explain me if anyone asks?'

'I'll tell them the truth, of course,' she replied. 'No point in doing otherwise if you intend staying.'

'Oh, I intend staying,' he told her. 'Wild horses wouldn't drag me away.'

'And would you be so definite about that if I wasn't going to give you another child? You never made any attempt to come looking for me before.'

'Maybe that's because I didn't know where you were. Nicholas is very good at clamming up when he has to. If you hadn't written to me everything would have been as it's been since...'

His voice trailed away, and she said gently, 'Saying his name isn't going to drag us back into the nightmare. I had to smile the other night. *Oliver Twist* was on television, and it reminded me of when Jamie was Oliver in the primary school Christmas play.'

He was laughing now. 'Yes, and how we thought he was miscast as he looked too well fed. I always thought he would have preferred to be the Artful Dodger.'

'And do you remember how they asked you to be the Father Christmas, and we were on pins in case he recognised you behind the whiskers?'

'Yes, I do,' he replied. 'I can still smell the glue that one of the teachers used to stick them on me.'

At that moment they saw the glint of water ahead, and as they stood beside the silent lake in the gloaming of a spring day, he said, 'You're right, Georgina. Willow Lake *is* beautiful.' He turned to observe her standing beside him with the so obvious signs of what was to come in her changing shape and thought, *And so are you.*

They walked back to Partridge Lane in silence, each wrapped in with their own thoughts, and when their cottages came into view, Georgina said, 'Thanks for doing the ironing. I could have been more grateful when you told me it was done.'

He was laughing and she observed him in surprise. 'What a mundane comment to end the evening after visiting that idyllic lake,' he said. 'If you leave me a key under the mat tomorrow and the vacuum cleaner handy, I'll carry on with the chores. Just make a list.'

'If it got around that you were my new home help, it wouldn't fit in with your image in the medical world,' she told him jokingly, and marvelled at the moment of rapport that had suddenly surfaced.

They were standing at her gate, ready to separate, and she wondered if Ben was waiting to be invited in for the rest of the evening, and if that was the case, what should she do? But it seemed there was no cause to concern herself about that. He was turning to go into his rented cottage and said over his shoulder, 'Goodnight, Georgina. Sleep well.'

'And you, too,' she said weakly.

He was smiling. 'I most certainly will…now.'

CHAPTER FOUR

WHEN Georgina was ready to leave the cottage the next morning, Bryan Timmins, the farmer who delivered her milk, was coming up the drive. Looking at the now-occupied place next door, he said, 'Do you think your new neighbour will want his milk delivered, Dr Adams?'

'I would think so,' she told him. 'The person in question is accustomed to getting it from the supermarket and won't have realised that he can get milk delivered.'

'So can I risk leaving him a couple of pints, then?' the farmer asked.

'Yes, I'm sure you can. I'll tell him it was my doing.'

'Who is he? Do you know?'

'Er, yes, I do. His name is Ben Allardyce. He's a paediatric surgeon.'

'Another doctor, eh?' With a change of subject, he asked awkwardly, 'And how are *you* keeping.'

'I'm fine, Bryan,' she told him. 'And what about *your* pregnant lady? I didn't see Maggie at the antenatal clinic last week.'

'No, you wouldn't. The wife has gone to her mother's for a visit before the baby comes. We can't wait. If it's a boy, young Josh wants us to call him after some pop star that he's keen on. I shudder to think!'

'And if it's a girl?'

'He hasn't come up with anything for that so far. Have *you* chosen any names yet?'

At that moment Ben's door opened and as he eyed them questioningly Georgina said, 'Ben, may I introduce Bryan Timmins, who supplies me with fresh milk every day?' As the two men shook hands, she explained, 'Bryan owns the farm that we passed when I took you to see the lake. I've taken it on myself to arrange for your milk to be delivered. Is that all right?'

He was smiling. 'Yes, of course, that would be fine. It would seem to be another of the delights of living here.'

The burly farmer laughed, 'Aye, it is, though it's not all moonlight and roses, you know. There's the worry of foot and mouth, for one thing which is every farmer's nightmare, though I've never had that to contend with so far. Then there are trespassers who don't keep to the designated paths and trample the crops of some of us, but all in all it's a good life and a happy one, living in the countryside. You think so, don't you, Dr Adams?'

'Yes, I do,' she agreed, knowing that Bryan had yet to discover the connection between herself and her new neighbour.

When he'd gone, Ben said, 'You're off early, aren't you, Georgina? It's only eight o'clock.'

'James wants a short practice meeting before the day starts.'

'I see. Would it be all right if I popped into the surgery later in the day to have a look around and maybe meet the senior partner?'

'Er, yes, I suppose so,' she said, taken aback at the fact he hadn't lost interest at the practice. It would be another part of her life here that Ben was invading if he got involved in the work there. 'How do you want me to introduce you?'

'However it suits you best,' he said calmly. 'Your next-door neighbour, a colleague from the past...or you could tell them the truth, that I'm your husband. You said it wouldn't bother you if people found out, as long as they don't get to know the reason why we split up.'

'But you're not my husband any more, are you?'

'Legally, no, but there are more important things than paperwork and documents.'

'Such as?'

'Do I have to explain?'

'No,' she told him hurriedly.

It was neither the hour nor the occasion to start delving into the past. She didn't think there ever would be a right time for *that*. If they had to live side by side for however long it took, she would abide by it, and if Ben was intending taking a major role in their baby's life, there wasn't much she could do about that, other than apply for sole custody, and she could not do that to him.

He had suffered enough, they both had, and after the hurt she'd caused by not telling him she was pregnant for so long, to do that would be rubbing salt into the wound.

'What time are you thinking of visiting the surgery?' she asked. 'Early afternoon is always quietest, when we're back from the house calls and have a lull before the second onslaught of the day.'

'Twoish, then?'

She nodded. 'I'll tell James that you're coming to look us over.' And without further comment, she went to start her day.

The staff meeting that James had called didn't last long. In essence it was to welcome Gillian and to tell them that he was going to delay appointing another permanent partner until his new brother-in-law came back.

They all dispersed to their various duties after that except for Georgina, who stayed behind for a moment and said, 'Is it all right if Ben comes to have a look around when we're quiet this afternoon? He's interested in everything that's going on here and has even suggested that he would be willing to help out until Glenn gets back from Africa.'

She'd said it as a kind of warning, in case Ben did say something to that effect, and James stared at her in surprise.

'Really?' he exclaimed. 'And is he qualified?'

'Er…yes. His name is Ben Allardyce. He specialises in one particular branch of medicine, but in the past he has been a general consultant as well.'

'Are we talking about *the* Ben Allardyce? The paediatric surgeon?'

'Yes. He is my ex-husband. I think he's decided that he's going to need something to fill the days while he's in Willowmere, and that's where the suggestion came from.'

'I would welcome him into the practice on a temporary basis with open arms,' James said. 'But how would *you* feel about it, Georgina?'

'I'm not sure. I wasn't happy when he first suggested it, as he's already renting the cottage next to mine, but we do need someone, James, and it will be even more urgent when I'm off after having the baby. So feel free to ask him, if you so wish.'

He was smiling. 'I do wish, Georgina. I'll have a word with him when he comes this afternoon—just as long you're sure that you'd be happy with the arrangement?'

'I think one of the reasons he's offering is because he wants to make it easier for me during the coming weeks, so how can I object?' she said, with the feeling that she might be losing her strength of will.

Leaving James to take in what could be good news for the practice, Georgina went to start her day.

Edwina Crabtree's test results were back and they were positive for the presence of Helicobacter pylori. Georgina requested one of the receptionists to ask her to come in to discuss the findings.

It was today that Christine Quarmby was seeing the first of the two consultants that she'd referred her to, she thought as patients came and went, and wondered how long the sick woman would have to wait for a result.

* * *

Ben arrived at exactly two o'clock and as she saw him come through the main doors of the practice with a positive stride, Georgina felt a sudden rush of warmth. He had been so dear to her once, she thought. How could she not want him back in her life again?

But remembering the hurts from the past, she was still unsure. His decision to stay in the village was because of the baby rather than her, and could she blame him for that?

He'd been a loving father to Jamie, and gentle with his small patients in the London hospital where he'd worked. He was a natural with children. So the thought of another one of his own to love was obviously bringing him out of the depression that he'd fallen into three years ago.

'Hi,' he said when he saw her coming towards him. 'As you didn't leave a key or the vacuum handy, I've cleaned all the outside windows, yours *and* mine.'

'Great, so I'll be able to see who's coming up the drive,' she said, smiling as if her mind wasn't filled with the whys and wherefores of him actually standing beside her in the village practice. 'You seem determined to make yourself useful.'

'It makes a change, don't you think?' he replied sombrely, and she had no reply to that.

James came out of his room at that moment and when she'd introduced them, he said, 'Shall I show Ben around the surgery, Georgina, or would you like to do the honours?'

'I'll leave it to you,' she told him. 'The nurses are taking the diabetic clinic this afternoon and it will be the first time for the new practice nurse so I thought I'd be around to assist.'

She was chickening out and knew it, but Ben had been the one who'd said he wanted to meet James and it hadn't been her idea that he help out in the surgery, so she left them to it with a murmured 'I'll see you this evening, maybe' in Ben's direction.

'Sure,' he replied easily, but there was a look in his eyes that said he got her drift.

She came out of the nurses' room when he was on the point of leaving and he said, 'Nice place you and James have got here, Georgina. The practice manager seems extremely capable.' Remembering Elaine's comments when she'd seen him walking past the window, she almost laughed.

Bringing her back to the present, he said, 'James said you mentioned my working here to him, and we've come to an arrangement. I was surprised when he told me, as I thought you weren't keen on the idea.'

'Shall we just say that I could see the advantages of it after I'd given it some thought? It will take some of the strain off me.'

'Why do you think I suggested it?' he said evenly. 'I'm going to drive into town for the rest of the afternoon and will probably eat out, so I'll see you tomorrow, Georgina.'

'Yes, whatever,' she replied, and went back to her patients.

James was on top form as they were leaving at the end of the day. 'Ben is coming into the practice full-time,' he said jubilantly. 'He's starting on Monday.

Aren't we the lucky ones to have someone of his calibre on the staff for a short period?'

'Yes, I suppose we are,' she said, and wondered if Ben really was coming to work there for her sake.

As she went for her usual short walk that evening, the fact that it would be Easter at the end of the following week came to mind. She had thought of going away for the weekend while the surgery was closed, but it was a lovely time in the village and an ideal opportunity to drive to London to put fresh flowers on the grave where so much of her heart lay.

The main thought in her mind was that she'd hurt Ben a lot by being so slow in telling him about the baby. Did she want to hurt him further by going to London without his knowledge? It would be as if she was putting him in his place again, the place where he had been for three long years.

The situation he'd created by coming to live in the village had a strong feeling of getting to know each other all over again, and it gave her a mixture of pain and pleasure. There was comfort in knowing he was near, knowing that she could see him, touch him, and that she wasn't going to give birth to their baby without him.

But his presence was threatening the life she'd built for herself in Willowmere. Her hard-won contentment was disappearing in her awareness of all the things she'd tried to forget about him. His smile, the mouth that had kissed her, the surgeon's hands, long-fingered and supple, that had caressed her, and the trim, hard strength of him that she'd always thought would be there to protect, as well as arouse her—these were all things that could weaken her resolve to stay alone if she wasn't careful.

In her most upbeat moments she felt as if what had happened between them on the afternoon when he'd finally caught up with her at the cemetery had been meant. That the fates had decided to give them a push in the right direction, but those kind of thoughts were always followed by memories of the months before she'd said goodbye to a wonderful marriage.

As she walked homeward through woods carpeted with bluebells, she decided that she would tell Ben that she was driving to London on Good Friday. If he wanted to do the same, he could make his own arrangements.

The thought of being closeted together in the car for hours on end would be too much for their frail reunion to cope with, as would being together as she arranged the white roses of innocence on the grave.

But there was the coming weekend to get through first. Saturday and Sunday would be days when both she and Ben would have time on their hands, which could prove awkward.

She went up to bed at her usual time and steeled herself not to listen for him returning. It paid off and she went to sleep not knowing whether he was back or not.

When she opened the curtains the next morning, his car was in his drive. She wondered how she would have felt if it hadn't been. If he'd given up on her and gone back to London, discouraged by her lack of warmth. But as she looked down at the part of her anatomy where their child was curled up safely she knew that the die was cast. Ben would never let this one out of his sight.

When he'd first appeared, she'd made it clear that he had no part in her life any more. She'd said it because she'd been afraid that he might try to take over when he found out about the baby. But now that he was settled in the cottage next door it seemed as if, having made his presence felt, he was easing off and she wasn't sure what to make of it....

She was planning to go into the town herself over the weekend to get some ideas on the requirements of a new baby as it had been nine years since she'd last been pregnant.

But first there was Friday ahead of her and when she arrived at the surgery, she saw Edwina Crabtree in the waiting room, looking more dour than usual.

'I'm afraid that we've had a positive result on the stomach infection, Miss Crabtree,' she told her when it was her turn to be seen. 'How is the neck pain?'

'Just the same.'

'And the indigestion?'

'No different.'

'Now that I know what I'm treating, I'm going to prescribe medication to treat the stomach problem which should soon give you some relief from the indigestion and the neck discomfort.'

'I hope so,' was the flat reply. 'Spring is one of the busiest times for we bellringers. Lots of brides want the bells to be pealing as they come out of our church, and because it is in such a charming setting it is one wedding after another from Easter onwards.'

Was that a nudge for her? Georgina thought wryly when she'd gone, that the baby she was carrying would benefit from the blessing of the church. It would seem that so far Edwina, like most of the inhabitants of Willowmere, was not aware that the child's father was now there.

When she arrived home that evening, Ben appeared the moment she got out of the car and said, 'I've seen a café sort of place near the post office. Do you fancy eating there tonight?'

'I suppose it's not a bad idea,' she agreed. 'It will be the Hollyhocks Tea Rooms that you've seen. We get lots of walkers stopping off in the village on the lookout for some good food as Easter approaches, and the Hollyhocks is the answer. The people who own it are friends of mine.'

'Does that make any difference? Are you sure that you'll be happy for us to be dining there if that's the case? Only I feel that we have things to discuss and in a place like that we're on neutral ground.'

'You make us sound like enemies.'

'I didn't mean to, but we're not exactly on the same wavelength, are we?' he commented dryly.

She didn't reply to that. What did he expect? They'd been living separate lives for the last three years. A week back in each other's company wasn't going to cancel that out.

'Give me a few moments to get changed and while I'm gone perhaps you could phone and make sure they have a table free.'

* * *

'So what is it that you want to discuss?' she asked when they were seated at a table by the window in the village's most popular place for dining without frills.

'I was looking at baby things when I was in the town yesterday—prams, cots and lots of other items our new arrival will need and...'

He'd seen her expression and didn't finish the sentence.

'You took it on yourself to do that without consulting me,' she said. 'I've thought a few times that since you found me pregnant, you see me as just a means to an end.'

The colour drained from his face but his voice was level enough as he said, 'If you'd let me finish, I was intending to suggest that we go shopping this weekend. No point being on the last minute with everything. But as you seem to think I've stepped out of line, maybe it isn't a good idea.'

Georgina felt the wetness of tears. He hadn't taken her up on her last comment but had taken it on board. She could tell by the set of his jaw and she wished she hadn't been so hasty. But it was all part of her uncertainty, the feeling of not being in control. Since coming to Willowmere she'd managed to achieve it to a degree, until the moment she'd seen him walking towards her in the lane.

Ben was reading the menu as if the subject was closed, but she couldn't leave it at that and told him, 'I was thinking of going shopping, too.'

'And were not intending consulting me from the sound of it.'

'I hadn't got any further than considering it. You've

not been here long, don't forget, and I'm used to doing things on my own, making my own decisions. I'm not going to get out of the habit in five minutes. I'm sorry if I upset you, but please don't rush me, Ben. By all means, let's go shopping together. We can order what we need on the arrangement that it is to be delivered once the baby has arrived safely.'

There was a question in the dark hazel eyes looking into hers. 'Why? Is there any reason why it might not, a problem that you've not told me about?'

'Not at present, but as we are both aware, sometimes things can go wrong.'

'What is it that you're not telling me, Georgina?' he persisted in a low voice.

'It's just that the gynaecologist is keeping a close watch on my blood pressure. It's all right at the moment. I check it all the time, but as we both know in pregnancies it can soon go sky high.'

'Who is this fellow?' he questioned. 'Does he know you had a difficult time with Jamie? I'll have a word with him to make sure he's knows what he's doing.'

She had to smile. 'You won't do any such thing. What about professional ethics?'

'Nothing is going to happen to this child if I can help it,' he said with a grim sort of calm that tore at her heart, 'and if it means checking up on the gynaecologist, I'll do it.'

'You're taking over again,' she reminded him. 'Ian Sefton is the best. I've made sure about that, Ben. Now, shall we decide what we want to eat? I'm starving.'

She'd introduced him to Emma and Simon, the

husband-and-wife team who owned the place, and now Emma was poised ready to take their order. Once that was done, they chatted about less personal things until the food arrived.

It was as they were strolling back home that Ben said, 'When is your next appointment to see this guy?'

'The week after Easter. You're not going to suggest that you go with me, are you? I'm quite capable of dealing with that part of the pregnancy myself.'

He sighed. 'Yes, I do know that. You don't really need me back on the scene, do you? You're extremely capable, but I'm afraid you are going to be lumbered with me. I feel we've been blessed with this little one that you are carrying and I'm sure you must feel the same.'

Tears were threatening again and she told him, 'Of course I do. How could I feel otherwise? But just give me time, Ben. It's been so long since anyone cared if I lived or died.'

'Silence doesn't have to mean not caring,' he replied. 'It's just that sometimes shame gets in the way.'

'We both did the best we could,' she said flatly.

'Yes, but mine wasn't good enough, was it?'

'We've done enough heart searching for tonight, Ben,' she protested.

'Yes, we have,' he agreed. 'Let's get you home and tucked up in bed with Baby Allardyce.'

Georgina had come to a standstill and he said, 'What's wrong? Are you all right?'

She was unbuttoning her jacket. Reaching out to take his hand, she placed it on to her expanding front and said in a low voice, 'Can you feel your child moving, Ben?'

'Oh, yes!' He looked at her, his dark eyes full of wonder. 'I can indeed. It's fantastic, Georgina.'

'Yes, it is,' she said softly. 'It keeps me awake sometimes, and when it does, I always wish I could share the moment with someone else.'

So he was just 'someone else', Ben thought sombrely. Not the beloved husband or the expectant father, but he wasn't going to be dismayed. In just a week they'd come a long way and every day was going to bring them closer together if it had anything to do with him.

Like tomorrow, which would be a big step forward when they went shopping together. It was all going to come right, he told himself. He just needed to be patient and maybe one day they might be a happy family once again. Nothing would ever replace Jamie, but there would be acceptance of it at last if he and Georgina could start fresh.

With regard to her antenatal appointment, Georgina would have to accept his anxieties. She'd had a difficult pregnancy when she'd been carrying Jamie. There had been problems with her blood pressure for most of the time, and she would not have forgotten *that*. He certainly hadn't. So far all seemed to be well, or she would have said, but he would be keeping a close watch.

They were happy and relaxed as they chose a pram, baby bath and a pretty white crib, along with a host of other things, and when they were paid for on the understanding that delivery would be made once the baby was born, there was only one moment of seriousness when Ben asked, 'How's the blood pressure?'

'Fine,' she said. 'You will be the first to know if ever it isn't.'

Once they'd finished shopping for the baby they strolled around the stores and dawdled until it was time for lunch. As they went to find somewhere to eat, Ben said, 'The other day I heard the farmer who brings the milk ask if you'd decided on any names for the baby. Have you?'

She shook her head. 'Nothing definite. Have you any ideas?'

'I might have. If it's a girl, how about Aimee? The French spelling of it?'

'We thought of that last time, didn't we?' she reminded him, and saw that he was smiling.

'Yes. We wanted Jamie for a boy, and chose Aimee for a girl because it sounded like Jamie without the *J*. What name would you choose for another boy?'

'Arran, maybe?'

'I like that. Arran Allardyce sounds good.'

They were waiting for a table to be free in a bistro in one of the stores, and after the brief discussion about names, silence fell on them.

Georgina was thinking that twice in the last few days Ben had been able to talk about Jamie as if he'd found some acceptance at last, and it warmed her heart.

Shopping together for the baby had been delightful. Having Ben beside her had felt so right. It had been like taking a step back in time to when all had been perfect between them, and now they were discussing names like any excited parents.

But they weren't like other parents, and they were going too fast. She needed some calm in her life while she adjusted to how it was going to be, instead of how it had been.

He was pushing it, Ben was thinking as he observed her closed expression. Why couldn't he have been satisfied with what they'd done together so far, without pinning Georgina down about names for the baby?

When they arrived back in Willowmere in the quiet Saturday afternoon, Ben noticed that cricket was being played on a field behind the vicarage. Observing the flashes of white against the fresh green of the pitch, he said, 'I might have guessed there would be cricket here. Does the village have a team of its own?'

'Yes, but today it will be just a friendly match as the season doesn't actually start until Easter, does it?' she replied.

'I might go to watch when I've dropped you off,' he said, 'or do you want to come?'

'No, thanks,' she told him with the feeling that she needed some time alone.

As if he'd picked up on something in her tone, Ben looked at her sharply. 'You've had enough of me for one day? Is that it?'

She shook her head. 'No. If you want to know, it's me that I've had enough of.'

He was stopping the car in front of their two cottages

and he turned to where she was sitting unmoving in the passenger seat and said, 'I'm not sure what you mean by that and am not going to ask. I'll see you later, Georgina. Why not have a rest while you have the chance?'

'I'll think about it,' she promised, knowing that she needed ease of mind as much as she needed ease of body.

The first person Ben saw when he arrived at the cricket match was James Bartlett with his two children, and the other man flashed him a welcoming smile. He was dressed in whites so was either a player or a stand-in, Ben decided, but as it was the interval at that moment and tea and cakes were being passed around, he couldn't tell which.

James had taken to this estranged husband of Georgina's, much to his surprise, as he'd been prepared to dislike the man who had obviously caused Georgina anguish in the past, but on meeting Ben he'd found him to be pleasant, intelligent, and a man he could communicate with.

What had gone wrong between them he didn't know, but he sensed an awareness of each other that told him feelings of some kind still ran strongly in them both.

'Do you play?' he asked the newcomer as he and the children took Ben to the pavilion for some refreshments.

He smiled. 'No. Not really. I used to play on the fathers' team when it was sports day at my son's school, and he and I used to play cricket in the back garden sometimes, but that's about it.'

James frowned in surprise. 'I didn't know that you and Georgina have a child. She's never said. Does he live with you?'

'No,' he said levelly. 'We lost Jamie in an accident when he was six years old. He was drowned.'

'Oh! I'm so sorry!' James exclaimed as Georgina's reserve and reticence were explained. He knew from bitter experience that some things just couldn't be talked about because they hurt too much, and it seemed that where he had lost a wife, Ben and Georgina had lost a child.

'It was losing him that broke up our marriage. Grief can be a cruel thing,' Ben said as one of the ladies behind the counter passed him a mug of tea. 'I take it that Georgina had never mentioned either him or me to you.'

'No, she hadn't,' James confirmed. 'So why have you come to Willowmere after all this time?'

'We met up by chance last August. I realised how much I still cared. She wrote to me some time ago, asking that we talk, but I was away and didn't get the letter until recently. I came here hoping for a reconciliation and discovered that she was pregnant, which means that I'm not budging. Whether she wants me here or not, I'm staying. I want to be there for her at the birth and afterwards. I let her down once when she needed me desperately and am not going to do it again.

'And do you know what, James? I've never talked to another living soul as I've talked to you today, but there is just one thing. Georgina is wary of me and I don't blame her, so could I ask you not to mention our conversation to her?'

'Yes, of course,' was the reply, 'and if ever there is anything I can do for either of you, Ben, you have only to ask.'

At that moment his children came up, asking for ice cream, and as Ben observed Pollyanna and Jolyon he thought that in spite of losing his wife the man standing beside him was truly blessed.

CHAPTER FIVE

WHEN Ben had gone to watch the cricket, Georgina lay on the sofa in her sitting room and thought about the time they'd just spent together.

They'd been happy as they'd chosen the baby's layette, perfectly in tune like any expectant parents shopping for an addition to their family. But now she was wondering if it was wishful thinking on her part. Theirs was a strange relationship, and where Ben seemed supremely confident that it was all going to work out, she was alternating between doubt and hope all the time.

The more she saw of him the more she craved to have him near, yet when they were together she was wary, and knew he sensed it. He'd asked her to watch the cricket with him and she'd refused because she felt that he was always one step ahead of her, taking her breath away and undermining her confidence in her own abilities at the same time.

He'd described her as capable, and most of the time she was, but not where he was concerned. What was

Ben expecting them to do once the baby had arrived? Set up house together as if the past didn't exist?

The sexual chemistry was still strong between them. It always would be. But she had to keep telling herself that there was more to a relationship than that. Understanding came high on the list.

She'd been taken aback when he'd wanted to discuss names for the baby. Obviously she'd given it some thought, yet had felt the time for that would be once it was born. Maybe he'd brought up the subject because today he was happy and relaxed like he used to be in the old days and now she was wondering if she was going to be able to live up to his expectations.

The phone trilled into her thoughts and when she picked it up it was Nicholas ringing from Texas, as he sometimes did.

After they'd exchanged greetings he said uncomfortably, 'I keep phoning Ben but there's no answer. He's been to Scandinavia, but I would have expected him to be back by now. I don't suppose he's appeared on your horizon, by any chance? He was desperate for your address before I left the country, but I kept my promise.'

She was fond of Ben's likable young brother and told him, 'As a matter of fact, Ben *is* here, and is intending to stay. He's over the moon because I wrote to him with my address, and when he turned up here he found that I was pregnant after we'd met unexpectedly in the summer.'

'That's fantastic!' he cried jubilantly, and then sounded less exuberant. 'But how do *you* feel about all this, Georgina?'

She sighed. 'I'm delighted about the baby, of course, but he and I haven't had a very good track record since we lost Jamie, have we?'

'Yes, but haven't I always said that the two of you belong together?' he said gravely. 'You can both be forgiven for losing the plot after something like that. Give it time, Georgina. On a more cheerful note, I *will* be over for the christening of my new nephew or niece. That is really great news.'

When he'd rung off, she thought that Nicholas was another optimist who thought it was going to be easy, but she was the one carrying the baby, the one who had fled from the aftermath of grief and vowed that she wasn't ever going to be hurt like that again.

With a sudden need for reassurance she reached for the jacket she'd taken off when she'd arrived home and, picking up her door keys, set off for the cricket ground.

James was batting at the wicket when she got there, but there was no sign of Ben amongst the spectators as she looked around her. She could hear children's laughter coming from behind the pavillion, and when she went to look, she smiled.

James wasn't the only one at the crease. There was another match taking place. Ben was the batsman, with a minuscule cricket cap on his head and a children's bat in his hands, pretending to brace himself against the tennis ball that Jolyon was about to bowl at him. Pollyanna was the wicket keeper behind a small set of stumps.

This is how he used to be, Georgina thought wistfully. It was turning out to be a day of turning back the clock.

When the ball hit the bat he flicked it high enough for Pollyanna to catch, and as the children gleefully shouted 'Out!' he turned and saw her behind him.

'This is a nice surprise,' he said. 'What made you change your mind?'

'I came to tell you that Nicholas has been on the phone and I've put him in the picture about what's happening here,' she explained. 'He's coming over for the christening.'

He laughed. 'That's great!' The children tugged at his arms, pleading with him to carry on with the game, and he gave her an apologetic smile. 'I won't be long. Are you going to sit and watch us?'

'I am, indeed,' she told him, with the appropriate amount of enthusiasm, and settled herself on one of the wooden seats that were scattered around the pitch.

They stayed until the match was over and the sun was sinking in the sky. As they were leaving, James said, 'The children want to know when you are going to play with them again, Ben. You've made a hit there.'

'Not with the bat,' he said laughingly. 'They're great kids, James.'

'They're a grubby pair at the moment,' their father said. 'It's going to be into the bath with them before supper.'

'He's a great guy too,' Ben said as James trooped off with a tired but happy child on either side. 'It's a pity he hasn't found them a loving stepmum.'

'I agree,' she told him. 'But James has yet to find

someone he can love as much as he loved his wife, and that's the problem. He would never marry for convenience. I firmly believe that one day the right woman will appear and everyone will be delighted.'

'If you feel up to it, why don't we offer to take the children out for the day some time soon, to give him a break?' he suggested. Partridge Lane came in sight and he glanced over at her. 'I've really enjoyed today. Shopping for the baby this morning and playing with James's kids this afternoon.'

'Yes, I can tell you have,' she said softly. 'Dare I remind you of something that used to make you really angry?'

'What?'

'Time really does heal. Doesn't it, Ben?'

'Yes, it does,' he agreed sombrely. 'But the scars remain.'

'They do, but we can live with them, can't we?'

'We have to,' he replied, and there was no bitterness in his voice.

In that moment she felt closer to him than she'd been in years. If they could have talked like this all that time ago they might have salvaged something from their marriage, she thought wistfully.

They arrived at their separate properties, and as they halted he said, 'As you arrived at the match shortly after I did, I take it you didn't have a rest?'

'Er, no, but I'm not an invalid, you know. It's like I tell my mothers-to-be at the antenatal clinic at the surgery—having children is a natural thing, to be taken in one's stride with common sense and pleasure.'

And what about high blood pressure and it's effects? he thought, but didn't voice it, even thought the memory was crystal-clear of the scares they'd had when she was expecting Jamie.

'Yes, of course it is,' he agreed. 'And I was not intending to fuss. I was merely going to suggest that I'll rustle up some food while you have a rest, if you are agreeable?'

'I'm agreeable,' she told him thankfully.

'I'll give you a knock when it's ready,' he promised as they separated.

Once Georgina was inside the first thing she did was check her blood pressure. The gynaecologist had warned her to keep a close watch on it, because it had been up slightly the last time she'd seen him.

However, today the readings were as they should be, and she breathed a sigh of relief.

On Monday morning of the week leading up to Good Friday, Georgina awoke to the knowledge that it was Ben's first day at the practice, and she was immediately wide-awake.

It was going to be very strange, she thought. They'd both been doctors all their working lives, but in different situations. She had always been in general practice and Ben hospital-based, so this was going to be the first time they'd worked together. She couldn't imagine what it was going to be like.

He was bringing in his milk as she was setting off, and he called across, 'I'll be right behind you.'

As she was pulling up outside the surgery she could see his car following, and felt her heartbeat quicken.

Georgina began to calm down as the day progressed. He was efficient, yet pleasant with both patients and staff. To the uninformed he was just another doctor at the surgery. James and Ben had arranged that all young patients should be passed to him, thereby receiving the benefit of his experience, and in any spare time that Ben might have he would share the general workload.

It was late morning before they had a chance to talk. He came out onto the forecourt of the practice as Georgina was about to set off on her home visits and said, 'James suggests that I tag along so that I can get to know the area better. Is that all right with you?'

'Yes, of course,' she told him. 'How's it going?'

'Fine,' he said easily, as if walking into a strange practice where his ex-wife worked was a doddle.

As she drove up the steep road that led to the moors and the peaks beyond, Ben wasn't missing a thing. 'It's rather remote and bleak up here, and very sparsely populated,' he commented as they drove the last mile to the tops. 'I could do your calls in these parts if you want.'

'No way!' she protested. 'The people who live in the cottages and farms up here are my friends.' She could have told him they were amongst those who'd made her welcome when she'd first come to Willowmere, lonely and lost.

At that moment a stray sheep came from nowhere. It ran across the road in front of the car and she had to swerve to miss it.

'Wow!' he exclaimed. 'Never a dull moment. The next time we have lamb for dinner I'll be asking where it's come from.' Suddenly his tone changed. 'Stop the car! There's someone lying beneath that outcrop of rock over there.'

'I see him,' she said, braking sharply.

By the time she'd eased herself out of the car Ben was bending over the motionless body of a man in walking clothes. He called, 'Fetch your bag, Georgina.'

Grabbing her bag out of the boot, she hurried over, fishing her mobile phone out of her pocket.

'Looks as if he's fallen over and hit his head,' he said, nodding towards the high face of rock beneath which he was lying. 'See the gash there on the side? I've got a pulse, but his breathing is shallow. We're going to have to get an ambulance up here, Georgina. Have you got a signal?'

'Thankfully. Right, I'm through.' She gave the information required and hung up. 'The ambulance is on it's way.'

Ten minutes passed. Ben and Georgina were monitoring the man's vital signs and Ben said grimly, 'They'd better hurry or we're going to lose him. Get ready to help me resuscitate, Georgina. OK, he's stopped breathing.'

They immediately began the resuscitation procedure. As the ambulance pulled up, the accident victim was breathing shallowly once more.

When the paramedics had gone, sirens wailing, Ben said, 'Phew! That was touch and go.' He turned to her as they walked slowly back to the car. 'Are you all right? It couldn't have been easy for you, crouching down beside him.'

'I'm fine,' she told him. 'Just relieved that we came upon the poor man. Do you think he stepped over the edge not realising there was a steep drop at the other side?'

'I don't know,' he replied. 'It's beautiful up here, but there can be dangers in this sort of rugged terrain. What would you have done if I hadn't been with you?'

'The best I could, I suppose. At least it's not snowing.' He was observing her sharply and, tuning in to the direction of his thoughts, she said, 'Don't worry, Ben. I've lived here long enough to know how to manage. Now, we'd better get moving or our next patient will think we've got lost. It's Ted Dawson at Summit Farm. His wife rang in to ask for a visit as he's got a lot of back pain and is barely mobile. Otherwise, knowing Ted, he would have come to the surgery as he's not one to make a fuss about nothing.

'The Dawson's are the most hospitable people. If I know Ellie, she'll be offering us homemade cakes and coffee.'

Ben's expression brightened.

'It's just a shame we won't be able to accept, as we're behind already with the home visits after what's just happened at Hellemans Crag.'

He groaned and said laughingly, 'So, do you think the farmer's wife could make us up a lunchbox?'

A barred gate leading to a farmyard had appeared in front of them, and they drove up to the farmhouse. After Georgina had introduced Ben to Ellie and Ted, they each examined the stricken farmer in turn.

After they had exchanged comments, Georgina told

the patient, 'We both think that you might have a slipped disc in your spine, Ted, but only an X-ray can decide that. We need to get you to hospital.'

Ted sighed. Looking around the pleasant farmhouse, he said, 'I can't afford to be off my feet in this kind of job, Georgina. Farming's not for stretcher cases.'

'I know,' she said sympathetically. 'So the sooner we get you sorted, the better, don't you agree? And in the meantime, can't those three sons of yours give you a hand?'

'They would if they were here,' Ellie chipped in. 'They're all at university now, but we'll sort something out until Ted is on his feet again.'

'Shall I pass the message around that Summit Farm can do with some help?' Georgina asked.

'Aye, if you would,' Ted said reluctantly. 'By the way, don't forget to have a cuppa and a piece of Ellie's cake before you go.'

'We'd love to, but I'm afraid we haven't time,' she said, and as they packed up, told them about the injured man they'd come across.

Almost on cue, Ellie said, 'So take a piece with you to eat in the car.' As Ben's amused glance met hers, Georgina knew she hadn't better refuse *that* offer.

'I can't believe that we dealt with a case of that kind on your first day at the practice,' Georgina said as they went to get their cars at the end of the second surgery. 'It would have been difficult if you hadn't been there.'

'So I *am* useful for something?' he said quizically.

'You're in a league way above the rest of us at the

practice, but don't make a big thing of it. It was great working with you, Ben.'

It was true, she thought as she drove home. Why couldn't she accept that living with him again could be just as good?

With the anxiety of working with Ben now having disappeared, Georgina still had to face telling him she was going to the cemetery on Good Friday, and it was approaching too quickly for her liking. Thursday was upon her almost before she knew it. She had to tell him that evening.

It was late in the afternoon, and on her way home she stopped off at the florist's on the main street of the village to pick up the white roses that she'd ordered earlier in the week.

As she came out of the shop, holding the flowers and smiling at something the girl behind the counter had said, she froze. Ben's car was parked behind hers and he was watching her through the window on the driver's side.

When she drew level, he wound it down and said levelly, 'I saw your car parked and wondered where you were. Could it be that you were intending to go to the cemetery and weren't going to tell me? What is it, Georgina? Don't you want me with you when you go there? Do you think I'm going to entice you back to the house again? I would never have expected you to be so unforgiving.'

'I'm doing what I've done at special times of the year,' she told him steadily. 'The only difference is that since I've been pregnant I've travelled by train instead of using the car. I'll be getting a local train from the station here in Willowmere early in the morning to connect with a mainline train from Manchester to London, if you want to come.'

'I do want to come, but I won't be going on this occasion,' he said, in the same sort of level tone. 'I've arranged to meet a colleague from Scandinavia. He's interested in the work I did out there, so we're spending the day together.'

His glance was on the perfection of the flowers she was holding. 'So, as I can't accept your lukewarm invitation, I'll make my own arrangements for visiting Jamie.' And, leaving her deflated, he pulled out from behind her car and drove off.

So much for her making a situation out of something that should have been handled tactfully, Georgina thought bleakly, and knew what she had to do.

Ben was home before her and when he answered her knock on the door, she said contritely, 'I'm sorry, Ben. I didn't mean you to find out like that. It was unkind of me.'

'So how did you want me to find out?' he asked dryly.

'I don't know!' she told him exasperatedly. 'I keep telling you that I'm used to doing things on my own.'

'And you want it to stay that way?'

'No. Not exactly, but the cemetery was the place where we met that day and since then nothing has been the same. Going together would bring back memories not just of our meeting there but what happened afterwards.'

'You don't want to remember that, then?'

She looked down at her unaccustomed width and wondered how he could ask such a question.

'I will never forget it as long as I live,' she choked. 'I have far more reason to recall it than you have.'

He stepped forward and touched her cheek gently. 'Yes, I know you have. Don't let me interfere in your routine regarding Jamie. Tell him I love him, and I'll come see him soon.'

'Yes, I'll do that,' she promised, 'but don't you think he knows? I won't linger in London. I expect to be back late afternoon...and maybe next time we'll be able to go together.'

It was five o'clock when the local train from Manchester stopped in Willowmere's small station and Georgina smiled as she stepped onto the platform, bright with its tubs and baskets of flowers. She could hear the jangling kind of music that told her the Easter fair had arrived. If Ben wasn't too late home, maybe they could have a wander around the sideshows and other attractions after they'd eaten.

So far he hadn't seen much of village activities and in a perverse sort of way she was keen to introduce him to country life, even though she was still adjusting to his presence.

The fair was a yearly event. Everyone turned out for it, and as she heard the noise of it she thought of tomorrow's wedding in the village. Edwina and her friends wouldn't be too thrilled at having the music from the fair drowning their efforts on behalf of the happy couple.

On the short distance to Partridge Lane it occurred to her that Ben in his present confident state of mind might suggest that they marry again, and if he did, what would she say?

There was no way she would agree for the sake of convenience or propriety. If she ever took his name again it would be because it was something she wanted with all her heart, and at the present time she didn't know what she wanted.

She wasn't to know that since yesterday his confidence had been at a low ebb. The fact that she'd intended going to London without him had been a sharp reminder that he'd blundered into the life that she'd made for herself, and she wasn't prepared to give it up so easily.

He arrived home at seven o'clock and the first thing he did was knock on her door to check if she was back. When she opened it to him, he observed her keenly.

'How did it go?' he wanted to know.

'Fine,' she told him. 'The trains were on time, no trouble getting a taxi. I spent an hour in the cemetery and then returned to Euston to get the train home.'

'And do you feel better for going?'

She smiled across at him. 'Of course. Need you ask? And now I've got a question for *you*. Can you hear the fair?'

'Yes. Where is it?'

'On spare ground beside the river. Shall we go once you've eaten?'

'I've already had something in Manchester,' he said. 'What about you?'

'I made a meal when I got in.'

'And you feel up to it.'

'Yes, but I don't think I'll be risking any of the rides. They do throw one about rather.'

'As your resident physician I agree that is good thinking,' he said lightly. 'I'll go and change into something comfortable and be back shortly.'

When they set off in the early April evening to where the fair had been set up, Ben thought that Georgina hadn't had much to say about her day except for the bare details. Remembering their discussion of the previous day, he decided she must be thinking that the least said would be soonest mended.

As they wandered around the various stalls and sideshows he won a soft toy for hitting the target on a shooting range, and when presented with a coconut for a good score at skittles, asked wryly, 'What are we going to do with this?'

Cries of alarm suddenly came from behind and someone shouted, 'Look out!'

They could hear the pounding of hooves coming towards them and as Georgina and Ben swung round the crowd behind them scattered as a white-faced teenage girl on a pony bore down on them with the animal out of control.

It took a split second for Ben to realise that someone was going to get hurt and that someone might be Georgina, and as the animal came charging towards them he grabbed the bridle. The impact almost wrenched his arm out of its socket and slammed him up against the supports of a nearby sideshow, but at least it had halted the frightened animal and no one in the crowd had been hurt.

The girl was shaking from head to foot. 'It was the music that made her bolt,' she said. 'I should never have brought Dinky near the fair but I couldn't resist, and nearly killed somebody.'

She turned to Ben. 'Thank you for saving me and my horse and some innocent person.'

He nodded. 'Fortunately no one was hurt, but another time do take care, young lady.' He smiled at her crestfallen expression. 'The next time you come to the fair, I suggest you leave Dinky at home.'

'I will,' she promised fervently, and with an apologetic smile for the onlookers rode off slowly towards a quieter part of the village.

Georgina was by his side, aware that every time he moved his arm and shoulder he was wincing, and she said, 'I'll take you to A and E to have your arm looked at.'

He shook his head. 'No, Georgina. I'm all right. Let's go home and I'll bathe it.'

'I'll bathe it,' she told him, and he smiled.

'All right, whatever you say. If it's still painful in the morning, I *will* go to A and E.'

When they got home she removed his shirt with gentle hands and saw a livid red weal across a shoulder that was already swollen and discoloured.

'Can you move it?' she asked anxiously.

'Yes,' he said calmly. 'It will be all right when the swelling goes down. I've just wrenched my shoulder joint.'

She was observing him doubtfully. 'I do think we should go to A and E to have it X-rayed.'

'I'll see how it feels when I've been in the bath,' he conceded.

'Let me put witch hazel on it first,' she insisted. 'It's so good for inward bruising and strains.'

As she rubbed the age-old remedy gently all over his back and shoulders Georgina was thinking that this was the first real physical contact they'd had since the day they'd made love. The opportunity to go back in time to when his wellbeing had been as important to her as breathing was a moment to treasure.

He was observing her whimsically over his shoulder and commented, 'I could really get to like this, though not the reason for it. That girl shouldn't have been anywhere near the fair with her pony. The kind of music they were playing was enough to frighten any animal. Someone could have been killed.'

He was reaching for his shirt and she said, 'Let me help you,' and held it out for him while he eased his arms into it. As she was pressed up against him, fastening the buttons, the baby moved inside her and she reached for his hand as she'd done on that other occasion.

It was a timeless sort of moment, yet in reality it only lasted seconds, and when it was over he reached out and took her face between his hands and kissed her gently on the mouth. Starved of the passion that had once been one of the mainstays of their life together, she kissed him back with a fervour that brought him rigid with surprise and pleasure.

When at last he put her away from him gently Ben said, 'I can't think of a better way of making me forget that my back hurts, Georgina. Does it mean that I'm forgiven?'

'I could say that I forgave you a long time ago,' she said breathlessly, 'but there was never anything to forgive. We just found ourselves travelling along different roads and there was nothing left to hold on to. But it doesn't mean that I've forgotten how it used to be.'

He was reaching out for her again but she shook her head and told him, 'As your doctor, I recommend rest and quiet. A repeat of what just happened is not in keeping with that. I suggest that you go home, have a warm bath and a hot drink, and we'll see how the patient is in the morning.'

'All right,' he agreed, and paused on the doorstep to comment dryly, 'I note that you managed to hang on to the cuddly toy. I wonder what happened to the coconut?'

When he'd gone, Georgina sank down onto the sofa and thought what a strange day it had been. It had started with her self-imposed solitary pilgrimage to London, followed by their visit to the fair that had changed from pleasure to panic in just a few seconds.

Then last, but by no means the least, in the emotionally charged moment that they'd shared after feeling the baby move, she had let her heart rule her head, given way to longing, and now she was feeling guilty because she'd given Ben cause to hope when she still wasn't clear in her mind about the future.

But exhaustion was kicking in and she went slowly upstairs to her lonely bed and tried not to think about how right it had felt when she'd been in Ben's arms.

As sleep began to slide over her she thought drowsily that it was almost as if the little unborn one, be it Aimee or Arran, was playing a little game of its own by making its presence felt at meaningful moments.

Next door Ben was having a leisurely soak to ease an aching shoulder and planning to sleep on the side not affected, wishing at the same time that he could awake the next morning to find Georgina beside him.

Outside in the lane in the dark spring night the fox slunk by once more on the lookout for an unsuspecting meal.

CHAPTER SIX

WHEN Georgina went to check on Ben's injured shoulder the following morning, he assured her that it was much better but, noting painkillers on the worktop in the kitchen, she insisted on being shown the affected area. When she saw the swelling and amount of bruising that had come out during the night, she said that they should have it looked at in A and E.

'I can move it all right,' he told her, 'so there is no fracture, but if you insist, I'll go.'

'*We'll* go,' she said. 'I'll drive.'

'*I'm* supposed to be looking after *you*,' he protested.

'I don't need looking after,' she told him firmly.

'So I've gathered, but don't forget when you go to see the gynaecologist next week, I *would* like to be there. What time is the appointment?'

'Three in the afternoon, between surgeries.'

She understood his concern. It had not been an easy pregnancy when she was expecting Jamie, but so far all was well, and she was not going to take any risks regarding the baby's safety. It was a precious gift, conceived in a moment of madness, and where at first she hadn't liked the thought of that, now she saw it differently because of the joy it was bringing with it.

Ben had been X-rayed in A and E at St Gabriel's, the main hospital for the area, and he'd been right. There were no broken bones, just a lot of soreness that could take a few days to ease off.

As they were about to leave, he said, 'I'm told they have a new paediatric centre here that is quite something.'

'Yes, they have,' she said.

'I know the manager of the unit. I'm sure he'll let us have a look round when he knows who you are.'

She was right. Ben's name brought immediate recognition, and they were shown round the centre by one of the doctors. Not only was it state-of-the-art, with every kind of up-to-date equipment, it was bright and sunny, with lots of things to take young patients' minds off their problems.

As they were leaving, Ben shook the doctor's hand and said, 'Many thanks for showing us round. My wife and I are most impressed.'

Georgina didn't comment on it when they left but he did. 'I know what you're thinking,' he said wryly. 'You're not my wife any more. I felt it more appropriate to introduce you like that as you are so obviously pregnant.'

'And so avoid any gossip?'

He glanced at her sharply. 'Yes, but on your account, not mine. I know what hospital grapevines are like. I don't give a damn what people think of *me*, but you are known in these parts.'

'Yes, I am,' she agreed levelly. 'I'm known as a woman who hasn't been open to any advances from members of the opposite sex since she came here, and who gets on with her life without burdening others with her problems and heartaches. Until you came back into my life James was the only one who knew anything about me and he has never heard the full story.'

'He has now. *I* told him,' he said coolly, stung by her words. 'I also told him that he was the only person I'd ever opened up to.'

She stared at him with surprised hazel eyes. 'When was this? You've barely met the man.'

'It was at the cricket match last weekend…and I like the guy.'

'Well! The new you is certainly full of surprises.'

They were back in the car ready to drive home and he said, 'Here's one more. I want to buy you an Easter egg like I used to when Jamie was with us, so can we stop off somewhere? Then we have to decide what we're going to do with the rest of the day. After all, it is Easter Saturday.'

Picking up on his mood, she said, 'I suggest we give the fair a miss after yesterday's near catastrophe. How about a picnic by Willow Lake?'

'Agreed as long as I help to prepare the food.'

She shook her head. 'No, rest your shoulder. I'll do the catering. I'll shop for it when we get back to the village and you can go on home and do your own thing for a couple of hours.'

And now she was making a salad to go with smoked salmon, and buttering crusty bread to be eaten with it before they went on to meringues and the apple tart that she'd bought at the village baker's.

As she bent to get fruit juice from the fridge, the Easter egg, resplendent in a fancy box with her name piped across in icing was there at her elbow, and she paused. Was she falling into a trap of her own making, allowing Ben to charm her with his concern and happy memories from the past when the future still wasn't clear?

'Do you remember how we used to call Jamie "Chocolate Chops" at Easter time,' he'd said, while they were waiting for her name to be piped on to the egg.

'Yes,' she replied softly. 'I remember everything the three of us did together, and I know that you do, too, Ben.'

It had been a tender moment that the girl behind the counter had broken into by saying laughingly, 'Your husband's name is Ben? That's a nice short name to go on an Easter egg. I've only just managed to get Georgina on yours!'

When Ben had bought Easter eggs for Jamie, he'd always bought one for her, and it would seem that he hadn't forgotten. In the pleasure of the moment she'd suggested the picnic and could hardly change her mind now, but for the rest of the holiday weekend she was going to retreat behind what few defences she had left.

When Ben had first arrived in Willowmere, she'd told him she didn't want a relationship with *anyone*, and had meant it. But she was realising that the bond between them remained unbroken. It might be battered and bent, but it was still there and always would be.

* * *

Next door Ben was also in a more sombre mood, remembering how Georgina had described herself at the hospital. He'd taken it on board at the time but pushed her words to the back of his mind. Now they'd come back to plague him and he wondered if they'd been a reminder that nothing had changed. That there might be precarious harmony between them but he wasn't to take it for granted. Her not wanting him with her when she went to see the gynaecologist fitted in with that.

Yet when she appeared carrying a picnic basket covered with a white napkin, she seemed happy enough, and he resolutely put his uncertainties to one side.

If the fair hadn't been in full swing at the other side of the village, Willow Lake would have been the star attraction on a sunny Easter Saturday, but as it was, there were just a few people there. Some out for a walk, others just sitting beside the water's edge, enjoying the peace of the place or having a picnic like themselves.

As Ben was opening up a couple of folding chairs and a small table that he'd taken from the boot of the car Georgina looked away and, seeing her expression, he asked, 'What's making you look like that?'

She managed a smile. 'Just a memory, that's all.' Before he could question her further, her attention was caught by the approach of Christine Quarmby, for once without her gamekeeper husband.

'Do I take the absence of your husband to mean there's a shoot taking place on Lord Derringham's estate?' she asked Christine after introducing Ben as her next-door neighbour and pretending not to notice the glint in his eye.

'Yes,' was the answer. 'His lordship has people staying with him over Easter, and Dennis is on call all the time. He wishes he wasn't as he's concerned about me, but I tell him that his job is our bread and butter, and I have to learn to be less reliant on him. It might sound ridiculous, Georgina, but I feel better now I know what is wrong with me.

'I'm not jumping for joy, far from it, but for anyone who is waiting for the results of tests and a diagnosis, it's like wandering in the wilderness. I've read all I can find about Sjögren's syndrome and searched on the Internet so I know the score. But it isn't going to stop me from leading as normal a life as possible.' She smiled at Ben, who had been listening intently. 'And now I'll go on my way having had my exercise for today.'

When she'd gone, he said, 'Is it secondary Sjögren's?'

'Yes. It stems from rheumatoid arthritis in Christine's case.'

'That's tough.'

'Yes, indeed. There is no known cure at the moment, but hopefully there will be one day.'

They'd left the picnic basket on the backseat of the car and now she went to get it and asked, 'Are you ready to eat?'

'Yes,' he said absently. 'It seems a long time since breakfast.'

His voice was flat. She sensed a change of mood in him and knew she wasn't wrong when he said, 'It isn't working, is it, Georgina? If I asked you to marry me a second time, what would you say?'

She was speechless with surprise. What had happened to his brisk confidence? Into the silence he said, 'You would say no, wouldn't you? You don't miss an opportunity to hammer it home that you were happier before I came on the scene. But I'm afraid I'm not going anywhere. You're going to have to endure having me here in Willowmere because the baby you're carrying is just as much mine as yours.'

She found her voice. 'What has brought this on?' she croaked. 'We've been getting on fine these last few days.'

'*I have,*' he replied. 'I can't vouch for you. I'm going to start looking around for a property to buy, so that our situation won't be so claustrophobic, and also so that when it's my turn to have the baby, it won't be in a bare rented house.'

'You've certainly been making your plans!' she exclaimed, unaware that he'd just said the first thing that had come into his head. 'So are you going to put the London house on the market?'

'No. We need somewhere close to where Jamie is, don't we?'

'You've certainly changed your attitude in the last couple of hours,' she said in a low voice. 'I'm sorry I haven't come up to scratch.' She got to her feet. 'I'll leave you to it as I've suddenly lost my appetite. I'll walk back. I need the fresh air.'

He was about to protest, but she didn't give him the chance, and as he watched her walk away beside the lake's clear waters he thought sombrely that if James's sister had fond memories of Willow Lake, *he'd* just spoilt it for Georgina.

He didn't stay long, ate some of the food without tasting it, then packed up and drove back to the cottage, taking note on his arrival that her car wasn't there.

She hadn't gone far. Georgina had driven up the hill road that led to the moors and was seated, gazing blankly in front of her, the car a solitary vehicle parked against the skyline, with the rugged grandeur of the peaks on either side.

Back there by the lake Ben had told her out of the blue that he'd given up on them being reconciled and it had taken hearing it put into words for her to acknowledge that her protestations that she wanted to stay as she was had been just a way of protecting herself from any more hurt.

She *did* want them to be a proper family again when the baby came. But Ben had taken on board what she'd said earlier, and as she'd been so definite, he'd had a change of mind. Now he was talking about buying a property in Willowmere that was not so close as they were now, *and* was in favour of them bringing up their child separately.

It was what she'd wanted at the start, because she'd been confused by his arrival in Willowmere, but the more they were together the more she wanted them to be like they'd been before. Instead she'd blocked every move he'd made towards that end. 'If I asked you to marry me a second time, you would say no, wouldn't you?' he'd said, without giving her the chance to reply, and now she was having to accept that she'd played the 'I am my own woman' card once too often.

If she were to tell him now that the answer would be yes if he asked her to marry him again, he wouldn't believe her. She could hear herself saying what sort of a woman she had become as they were leaving the hospital that morning. Warning him once again that she wasn't going to fall into his arms and take up where they'd left off three years ago.

So, what now? she thought miserably. The sensible thing would be to carry on as normal. It was just a matter of weeks before she gave birth and that was the most important thing in both their lives. If afterwards Ben kept to his word and moved out of their close proximity, she would have to console herself with the knowledge that at least he was in Willowmere, and accept that once they were parents again, she might be the one who had to do the begging.

When she arrived back at the cottage, Georgina saw that Ben had returned and she hurried inside, only to have to open the door to him seconds later and find him on the step, holding the picnic hamper.

'You haven't eaten since this morning, have you?' he said, bringing the moment down to basics. 'So why not make use of this?' Placing it in her hands, he turned and went without commenting that she should be eating for two, but she was pretty sure that was what he was thinking.

She stayed in for the rest of the weekend, saw Ben drive off and return a few times but he didn't call again, and when Easter was over, she set off for the practice on Tuesday morning, grateful for the chance to be near him.

As she waited for her first patients to present themselves, she thought that it was typical of life's twists and turns that when Ben had joined the practice she'd thought it wasn't a good idea from her point of view. Now his presence there was assuming the proportions of a lifeline, if only he would come out of his consulting room and say something.

As if he'd read her thoughts, the door across the passage from hers opened and he was there, smiling a tight smile and asking dryly, 'How was the Easter egg?'

It was hardly what she'd expected to be the first topic of conversation when they came face to face again, but she held on to her composure and said, 'I've eaten the George part and saved you the Gina bit. Perhaps you'd like to call round for it?'

'Yes, perhaps I would,' he said, unconvincingly, and she thought that the gap between them was widening. Then he asked, 'What arrangements have you made with James for tomorrow, when you see the gynaecologist?'

'I'm taking the afternoon off. Are you coming?'

'Yes, I'm coming. I thought we'd sorted that? I'll have to meet you there, though, and come straight back, as it will be two doctors missing from the surgery all afternoon if I don't.'

'Yes, whatever is best for the surgery,' she agreed.

It was a moment to tell him that she really *did* want him there beside her when she saw their baby on the scan, but if she told Ben that he might find it hard to believe after what had happened between them at that travesty of a picnic.

As Michael Meredith seated himself opposite her minutes later, Georgina wondered what had brought the local celebrity to the surgery. The man was a well-known botanist turned writer who wrote about the flora and fauna of the countryside and was something of a recluse.

Unmarried and in his sixties, he was rarely seen at the surgery, but today he had made an appointment for some reason that she was about to discover.

He was a pleasant man with a well-modulated voice and open expression, and as they exchanged smiles she asked, 'What can I do for you today, Mr Meredith?'

'I'm in severe pain at the bottom of my back and down my right leg, Dr Adams,' he informed her. 'I was clambering over some rocks to get a rare specimen a couple of days ago and slipped and jarred my hip. Within a short time the pain came and it is the kind of agony one can't ignore.'

'If you would like to lift your shirt and loosen the belt of your trousers, I'll take a look,' she told him. After examining his lower spine, right hip and knee, she said, 'I think you might have damaged the sciatic nerve which is the biggest nerve in the body. It passes behind the pelvis, then backwards to the buttock, from where it runs behind the hip joint and down the back of the thigh. When it reaches the knee, it separates into two separate nerves, known as the tibial nerve and the common peroneal nerve, and the pain that you've described are in those areas. In the meantime I'll give you some strong painkillers and a letter to take to the radiology department at St Gabriel's and they'll X-ray you while you're there.'

'What, straight away?' he exclaimed.

'Yes. You might have to wait a little while but it will be done on the spot. I should get the result within the week and in the meantime don't go rock climbing.'

He was smiling as he got up to go. 'There's no likelihood of that in my present state.'

Or in mine, Georgina thought as the botanist bade her goodbye.

When Beth came round with a tray of coffee in the middle of the morning, she said, 'You don't look very chirpy this morning, Georgina. Pregnancy gets wearying towards the end, doesn't it? And the hormones start playing tricks. One moment the mother-to-be is happy, and the next she's all droopy.'

'That decribes me exactly,' she told Beth, but knew her depression wasn't anything to do with hormones.

As she came up the lane that evening, drenched by a sudden downpour that had caught her unawares on her solitary stroll, Ben's door opened and they came face to face for the second time in the day.

'You're wet through!' he exclaimed, taking in the vision of her hair lying damply against her head and the loose dress that she'd changed into when she'd arrived home from the surgery clinging to her ample waistline.

'Yes, I do know that,' she said wryly, 'and I didn't do it on purpose, so if you'll excuse me, I'll go and change into some dry clothes.'

'And then will you come back for a moment?'

'Er, yes, if you want me to,' she agreed doubtfully, 'but I don't want a lecture.'

'You won't get one,' he promised quickly. 'And now will you go and get out of those wet clothes? I can't run the surgery on my own if you get pneumonia.'

'Yes, all right,' she agreed flatly. 'I'd hate to be a nuisance.'

She was unzipping the dress even as she opened her front door and as soon as she was in the hall stepped out of it and then went to towel her hair dry.

Exhaustion always seemed to creep over her at this time of day and, instead of changing into fresh clothes, Georgina wrapped herself in a warm robe and padded across to the house next door.

When she'd left him by the lakeside, Ben had forced himself to stay where he was. He'd wanted to chase after her and give Georgina the chance to reply to his outburst, but hadn't done so because he'd believed he was right and her abrupt departure had only added to that feeling.

They'd been in harmony for days until she'd outlined what she wanted from life as they'd been leaving the hospital, and it had made him see that they were not going anywhere as a couple.

It had been a pleasant enough moment when he'd taken her to buy an Easter egg, and when she'd followed it up with the suggestion that they have a picnic, he'd been all for it, but it hadn't stopped him remembering what she'd said before that. It had kept going round and round in his mind and his optimism had suddenly been in short supply.

Now he was regretting letting it show, as instead of bringing everything out into the open it had made the future more uncertain, with the only thing to hold on to being the arrival of the baby.

'You're tired,' he said when he opened the door to her.

'Yes,' she agreed, and thought she wasn't just that, she was miserable and lost and lonely. Her time was drawing near and she had no stable plans for the future. She'd known where she'd been heading before Ben had come to Willowmere. Had been ready to step into the role of single mother, but his coming had changed all that.

Just as she'd been beginning to accept that there could be a second chance of the family life that had been so important to them in the past, she'd driven Ben away by harping on how she was content with her lot as a woman alone.

Unaware of her heartsearching, he was trying to think of a reason for asking her to call back after she'd dried out. The truth of it was, he just wanted to be with her for a while, without the trappings of the surgery around them.

'I've made a hot drink to warm you up after the soaking you got,' he said. 'It can get chilly once the sun goes down.'

'Thanks for that,' she told him, feeling some of the chill of her body and mind disappear at the first sign that Ben might be relenting.

'How's the blood pressure?' he was asking, and she flashed him a pale smile.

'All right so far. It's the first question Ian will ask tomorrow afternoon.'

'Talking about blood pressure going up, ours in particular, do you remember that poor guy who'd fallen down the rock face?'

'Yes, of course I do.'

'When they got him to A and E they discovered he'd suffered a subdural haematoma from the fall and had to operate on him smartly.'

'And how is he now?'

'Doing all right, from what I can gather. I had to do a bit of pulling rank when I rang the other day to ask how he was, with my not being a relative, but the sister in charge mellowed when she knew I was one of the doctors who'd treated him up on the tops.'

'Why didn't you tell me before?' she asked, her eyes questioning above the rim of a mug of hot chocolate.

'Why do you think?' he asked dryly. 'I've been giving you the space that you are so keen to have.'

She put the mug down and got to her feet, too tired to get involved in emotional matters. 'Thanks for telling me about the walker.' She didn't comment on his last remark because it had been partly true. She did want her own space and she always would. But she wanted him more.

'What was it that you asked me to come back for?' she asked from the doorway.

'I just wanted to confirm the arrangements for tomorrow. I'll try to be there for quarter to three,' he said, improvising quickly, and with a brief nod, she went.

* * *

Once again sleep was long in coming, and as she lay wide-eyed beneath the covers, Georgina was thinking about how Ben's patience and understanding had been easing her into a new beginning after his arrival in the village, and now it had all fallen apart. They desperately needed a better understanding. Perhaps seeing the baby on the scan tomorrow would be a step towards it, but Ben wasn't one for going back on his word.

When she arrived at the consultant's rooms at a quarter to three there was no sign of him. Her heart sank, but maybe she was being a bit previous. There was still time for him to arrive.

She was beginning to feel weepy and vulnerable as the minutes ticked by and he still didn't appear, but consoled herself with the thought that it was because her hormones *were* all over the place as Beth had suggested, and there were other body changes to contend with, too. So by the time she was shown into the presence of the gynaecologist, she was resigned to the fact that Ben wasn't coming. All the fussing and insisting that he was going to be there had been for nothing.

Ben had arrived on time but, having parked his car, had just crossed the busy main road to get to the large Victorian building that housed the private rooms of various consultants when a young boy walking in front of him with his mother had gone into a fit.

It had appeared to be the first time ever, as the woman had been transfixed with shock. Ben had been beside them in an instant, loosening the child's clothing and checking that his tongue hadn't gone back and blocked the airway.

'We mustn't move your boy,' he'd told her. 'He will come out of it gradually. Has he had a convulsion before?'

'No, never,' she sobbed.

'I'm going to phone for an ambulance,' he announced. 'I'm a children's doctor and I will stay with you until they get here. Try not to be too alarmed. He won't remember a thing when he comes round. But he needs to be taken to hospital to be examined.'

He was glancing at his watch. It was ten minutes past three. Georgina would think he wasn't coming. The woman had seen him checking the time and begged, 'Don't leave us. I'm terrified. I've never seen anyone in a fit before.'

'I won't leave you,' he promised, and prayed that the ambulance wouldn't be long. It came in ten minutes, but it took another five for him to feel he could safely leave the woman and the boy, who was now coming out of what was very likely to be an epileptic seizure.

He ran the rest of the way and told Ian Sefton's receptionist, 'I should have met Georgina Adams here at three o'clock, but have been delayed. Is she in with Dr Sefton now?'

'Yes,' the receptionist said. 'I'll buzz him and let him know that you've arrived.' After doing so, she looked up and smiled. 'You can go in, Dr Allardyce.'

'I'm so sorry,' Ben said as he faced Georgina and the consultant. 'A child in front of me on the street had a seizure as I was approaching this place. His mother was almost hysterical and I just had to stay with them until an ambulance came. Have I missed the scan?'

Georgina was smiling. Ben had come after all. He'd always been a man of his word. How could she have doubted him?

'All is well with the baby and mother,' Ian Sefton told him. 'I will show you both the scan in a moment, and you will see that the head hasn't yet moved down into the pelvis. That is normal enough in a woman who already has had a child. So now the picture show, which I'm sure you must be eager to see. There is your baby,' he said, and they gazed enraptured a the image.

Georgina reached out and took Ben's hand in hers, saying in a low voice, 'I thought you weren't coming and I'm ashamed.'

'Don't be,' he told her huskily, with the wonder of the moment sweet upon him. 'We've made a child, Georgina, and we're going to give it all the love that we never got the chance to give Jamie.'

'I want to see you again in a fortnight now that you're into your third trimester of the pregnancy,' the consultant was saying. He turned to Ben. 'I've checked the blood pressure myself, even though as a doctor Georgina is quite capable of monitoring it, and at this stage I'm satisfied there are no problems coming from that direction. I know that she had a difficult pregnancy with your first child, so I'll be keeping a keen eye open for any signs of hypertension.'

When they'd left the building, and were going to their separate cars, Ben said, 'I'm relieved that so far your blood pressure is behaving itself. I've been dreading…'

He hadn't put it into words, so she said it for him. 'That we might lose this child as well?'

'It just seems too good to be true. Everything does.'

'Not quite everything,' she said gravely, and as she wasn't going to beg, got into her car and set off for Partridge Lane, leaving Ben to make his way back to the practice for the rest of the afternoon.

She didn't see him that evening, which was something of an anti-climax after those incredible moments at the gynaecologist's. Having the afternoon off meant that she ate earlier than usual and had her walk earlier. She'd expected that he would be home by the time she got back, but there was no sign of Ben's car on his driveway. Feeling tired and disappointed, she decided to go to bed.

When she'd undressed and put on the roomy night-dress that he'd once ironed for her, Georgina stood motionless by the wall that separated the two cottages. The longing to have Ben beside her through the night was so strong she felt that he must surely sense it on the other side of the wall.

But nothing moved. There was no knock on her door or urgent ringing of the phone and, turning away, she climbed slowly into bed. It was as she placed her head on the pillow that she heard it and it was not the kind of sound she was longing for.

There was hammering coming from the other side

of the wall and the whirring of a hand drill, and she thought wryly that Ben's thoughts must be a million miles away from hers if he was putting shelves up or hanging pictures.

Since he felt that they still had separate agendas for the future, Ben found the evenings never-ending with Georgina next door, so near physically yet so out of reach in every other way. He needed something to occupy himself with and had decided he was going to fill the empty hours by making a cot for the baby.

They'd bought a crib but he knew that infants soon outgrew their first sleeping place and the thought of their child lying in a cot that he'd made for it was appealing. He'd bought all that was needed for the venture on his way home and was now hard at work in the spare bedroom, unaware that the noise of his labours could be heard through the thick stone walls of the cottage.

'What were you doing last night, putting shelves up?' Georgina asked the next morning as they were about to leave for the surgery in their separate cars.

'Why? Could you hear me?' he exclaimed. 'I'm sorry if I disturbed you.' Intending that the cot was going to be a surprise, he replied, 'No. I was repairing a loose floorboard.'

'Oh, I see,' she replied, and let the matter drop.

CHAPTER SEVEN

AS THEY drove to the practice they passed Jess, the nanny, taking James's children to school. When they arrived at the surgery, Georgina said, 'Are we going to do as you suggested and take Pollyanna and Jolyon out for the day?'

He didn't reply immediately and she wondered if he was remembering Jamie and thinking that he was always involved with other people's children, never his own. Yet surely the baby she was carrying was going to take some of that kind of ache away? And it had been Ben's idea in the first place.

He was observing her thoughtfully, and she wasn't to know that his hesitation was on her behalf. She was nearing the end of her pregnancy, had a demanding job at the practice, and should be resting whenever possible. But he knew what Georgina would say to that. It would be the same thimg she said to the women at the antenatal clinic at the surgery. Pregnancy was a natural thing, not an illness. But with regard to the woman he adored there was the spectre of possible blood pressure problems in the background.

He longed to hold another child of theirs in his arms,

but she came first. Three long and lonely years had shown how much she meant to him, and he'd resigned himself to accepting it if she didn't want him back in the fullest sense. As long as he could be near her and the baby when it came, so that he could watch over them, he would stay on the fringe of their lives for ever if he had to. It would be better than nothing.

She was waiting for an answer. 'Yes, if you like,' he said with assumed easiness. 'But only if you feel up to it and whatever we do isn't too strenuous.'

'I'll mention it to James, then. How about this coming Saturday?'

'Fine by me,' he said, unable to stop his spirits from lifting at the thought of spending some prime time with her. 'Where should we take them?'

'There's a stately home not far from here that gets lots of visitors. The inside is full of beautiful pictures and antique furniture, which wouldn't be of much interest to Pollyanna and Jolyon, but in the grounds there are brilliant amusements for children and lots of animals for them to see. Once we've done the rounds, there are grassy slopes where visitors can picnic if they don't want to use the restaurants.'

'That sort of place would be ideal for keeping a couple of youngsters happy for a few hours,' he agreed. 'Hopefully the picnic will be an improvement on our last one.'

'Thanks for reminding me of the day you gave up on me,' she said quietly, and preceded him into the roomy stone building that was the centre of healthcare in the village.

* * *

'That would be great,' James said, when Georgina aproached him about having the children for the day. 'It will give me the chance to do a few things I haven't been able to get to for ages. What time shall I have them ready?'

'Ten o'clock, shall we say? It will take us an hour to get there.'

'They'll love it,' he enthused. 'Especially if Ben is there. Don't be surprised if Jolyon turns up with his cricket gear.'

'I never did find out where Ben got that cap from,' she said laughingly.

'It probably belonged to one of the junior team and had been left hanging around the pavillion.' He smiled.

Georgina was smiling too as she drove to the local children's boutique, a small but classy place called Ribbons and Rompers. The owner, Tessa Graham, had asked for a visit. After leaving James to his own activities, she was making the shop her first stop.

When Georgina arrived there, she saw that the shop blinds were still down and there were no signs of life around the place. She rang the bell outside a door at the bottom of stairs that led to an upstairs apartment, and it was a few moments before it was opened. Tessa was revealed hunched in a towelling robe and looking pale and listless.

As she led the way upstairs the shopowner said weakly, 'I've got the most awful stomach cramps, Dr Adams, and have been vomiting and had diarrhoea for most of the night. I think I passed out once. I found myself on the bathroom floor and don't recall how I got there.'

'It sounds as if you might have food poisoning,' Georgina told her, 'or a severe gastric upset of some sort.' She was looking around her, could see into the kitchen and it was spotless, as was the rest of the apartment.

'Have you eaten anything in the last twenty-four hours that could be suspect?' she asked.

'I went to a barbeque last night and had some sausage that could have done with being cooked a bit longer, but apart from that I can't think of anything else that could have caused it. I'm usually very fussy about what I eat.'

'Maybe not fussy enough this time,' Georgina suggested. 'It could be the sausage that has caused this, so don't eat any food until you haven't been sick or had diarrhoea for several hours, and then only small amounts of very plain food. In the meantime, try small sips of water and gradually build up your fluid intake. Make sure you drink regularly. The only comfort to be had from this sort of thing is that once the stomach has emptied itself and the colon likewise it can only go on for so long and then it must be allowed to settle. Send for me again, Tessa, if the symptoms persist or get worse, but I think it will have been the sausages that have upset you.'

When she arrived back at the practice, Ben was closeted with a patient. As soon as he was free he asked, 'Have you spoken to James?'

'Yes, he's happy for us to have the children for the day.'

And are we sticking to plan A?'

'Yes, and I think we should pray for good weather as these dry, sunny days aren't going to last for ever.'

He nodded, and in a more serious tone said, 'Have you decided what you are going to do about the practice when you have the baby? Are you going to take the full maternity leave? I can't believe we haven't discussed it.'

'That's because of the confusion in our lives,' she told him. 'But you're right. It needs to be sorted.'

'So why don't I take you out for a meal tonight and we'll talk about it while we're relaxing? It will save us having to cook.'

If he thought she was going to be relaxed while they were discussing the future, Ben was very much mistaken. But the idea of dining together, as they'd done a few times when he first came to the village, was appealing, and she said, 'Yes, that would be nice.'

James had overheard the conversation and said, 'There is something that has just cropped up that might influence your plans, or otherwise. You know that I wouldn't want to lose you, Georgina, as the practice wouldn't be the same without you, but if you decided you wanted a break from work until your little one is older, I've had a registrar from St Gabriel's on the phone. He wants to move into general practice and as his contract with the hospital is up at the end of May, he asked if there was any likelihood of a vacancy in Willowmere.

'His name is David Tremayne and he met Anna and Glenn in A and E last winter on the day when there was a near tragedy on Willow Lake. It was frozen over and when the ice began to melt someone fell through and nearly drowned.

'It must have stuck in his mind and he's coming in for a chat. He sounded a very capable guy but, Georgina, I want us to do what is best for you. So let me know once you've decided. And enjoy your meal.'

She smiled. It would be great just getting dressed up and going to a nice restaurant, but the real pleasure would be in the opportunity to spend some time alone with Ben. If only he felt the same as she did, she would stand over a hot stove if she had to.

When he'd first come to Willowmere, he had been desperate for her company. Now it was just the opposite. It was she who longed for his, but ever since he'd said that it wasn't working out between them, it had been in short supply socially.

She was seeing plenty of him at the surgery but that was a different ball game. They were there to work.

When she opened the door to him dressed in a long black skirt and a low-necked top, relieved by a silver choker, he said, 'Very nice! It reminds me of how it used to be before we were married. You opening the door of your parents' house to me all dressed up for the evening ahead. You're a beautiful woman, Georgina.'

She patted her midriff laughingly and questioned, 'Like this?'

'Yes, like that. Pregnancy suits you.'

'Next thing you'll be saying I should try it more often,' she teased, still in a light-hearted mood, but his reply was serious.

'I suggest that we focus on getting *this* little one safely into the world.'

'Yes, of course,' she told him. 'I've started putting my feet up for half an hour each evening when I get home.'

'They're not swelling, are they?'

'Just a little, but they'll be down by morning.' She pushed him gently to one side as she locked the door, and then they were off.

'So where are we heading?' she asked half an hour later as Ben turned the car onto the hill road in the dusk of a spring night.

'A new place that was recommended to me by a patient,' he explained. 'It's described as a farm restaurant and she said the food was delicious.'

'Ah! I know it!' she exclaimed. 'I noticed it when I was up there visiting a patient a few weeks ago. I remember thinking that someone had invested a lot of money in it, considering that it's rather out in the wilds.'

'Yes, that may be, but don't you think that people are prepared to travel miles for some good food?'

As they were shown to a table in a tastefully presented dining room that was already half-full, it seemed as if Ben's comment that the population would travel far for some good food had been correct. When it was put in front of them, they had their answer in succulent steaks and crispy home-grown vegetables.

They ate silently and with relish after a long and busy day, and it wasn't until they were relaxing over a coffee for Ben and a herbal tea for Georgina that she said, 'Until you came I intended to take full maternity leave from the practice, for obvious reasons. I was on my own, and I didn't think I could bear to leave the baby in someone else's care any sooner than I had to. If that someone was you it would be a different matter. But now you're involved in the practice as much as I am.'

'I don't have to be if James takes on another doctor. He might decide to do that if this registrar from St Gabriel's is the right man for the job.'

'You said you were going to look for a property,' she reminded him. 'That could affect any arrangements we made—especially if it was out of the area.'

As if! Everything he cared about was here in Willowmere.

'Have you seen anything suitable?' she continued.

'No, not yet. I haven't had a lot of time for house-hunting so far.'

She nodded. 'The weeks are speeding past. Some-times I can hardly believe that I'm carrying our child and will soon be giving birth.'

He didn't have that problem, Ben was thinking. The baby was always in his thoughts. *As was his beautiful wife.*

Ever since he'd found out that Georgina was preg-nant it had been like stepping out of darkness, but it wasn't stopping him from feeling that he didn't deserve it after the way he'd acted in the past. Calm, clinical doctor that he was, neither did it prevent him from waking up in the night with the dread in him that some-thing could go wrong.

After they'd seen the scan at the gynaecologist's rooms, Ian Sefton had phoned him that same night, and he'd been tense as a violin string when he'd heard his voice at the other end of the line. But it had been merely a social call to say that until he'd seen them together he'd had no idea that he was the father of Georgina Adams's baby.

'She *was* my wife once,' Ben had explained in clipped tones, 'but we lost our little boy in a tragic accident and our marriage broke down.'

'Sadly, that can happen,' the other man had said gravely. 'But you're back together again and starting a new family, which has to be good. Before I take up any more of your evening, the reason I called is because I'd very much like to chat with you some time. I'm a great admirer of your work, and often paediatrics and gynaecology walk hand in hand.'

'Yes, why not?' he'd agreed. 'Some time after the baby is born, perhaps.'

'You're not listening,' Georgina was protesting.

'Sorry. I was thinking about a phone call I had from Ian Sefton the other night.'

'Not about me, I would hope!'

'No. That would hardly be ethical, would it? He wants me to meet up with him when it's convenient, to discuss our respective professions.'

'That's nice.'

'Yes, I suppose so. Let's talk about babycare. There are a few options open to us. My staying at home while you go back to work is one of them. It would give me lots of time with the baby.'

'I wouldn't want you to do that,' she told him.

He stilled. 'Why?' *Because I'm not really your husband?* he thought.

'Ben, your skills are too important to be hidden away. I know there are times when you feel that your life is full of other people's children instead of your own, but those same children need you. You can't disappear out of their lives.'

'So what, then?' he questioned.

'I don't know. James isn't rushing me into a decision now that he's got you, and if you want to go back to what you do best he will still have David Tremayne in the practice, which gives me ample time to decide what my future role in it will be. It will depend largely on what sort of arrangements we make for the future.'

Georgina was giving him an opening, but he remained silent, and her hopes faded. It seemed that Ben hadn't changed his mind. They were going to be together, yet apart, with just one precious bond to bind them.

With the departure of the sun that had beamed down on Willowmere during daylight hours there was a chill in the air when they left the restaurant and Georgina shivered in the flimsy clothes she was wearing.

Ben had seen the shudder and was already taking off his jacket and draping it around her shoulders protectively. The simple, caring gesture brought tears to her eyes.

He saw them and wanted to know, 'What's wrong?'

'Nothing,' she told him, managing a watery smile, and thought that their lives were full of contradictions.

When he turned the car into Partridge Lane, she said hesitantly, 'Would you like to come in for a nightcap?'

Of course he would like to! He would *like* to go inside with her and stay there for evermore he thought, but he knew that Georgina was still holding back. He'd lost her trust once and she wasn't going to risk any further heartbreak even though the bond was still there.

In his most despondent moments he told himself that if it hadn't been for the baby, she would have sent him away long ago, but almost as if by divine providence they'd been given something to unite them in joyful anticipation.

'No, thanks just the same,' he said easily, trying not to choke on the words.

She nodded as if that was the answer she'd been expecting, and went inside.

When they went to call for Pollyanna and Jolyon on Saturday morning, the children were watching for them from the window of Bracken House. When James opened the door, he said, 'These two young ones have been looking for you ever since breakfast-time and are bursting to know where you're taking them.'

'We're going to a place where there are lots of animals and exciting things to do,' Ben told them. 'We're going to have a picnic while we're there, as well.'

Georgina smiled as the children, with eyes like saucers, listened to what he had to say.

'You'll have hit the jackpot with that,' James said.

Pollyanna was hopping with excitement, but Jolyon,

always the deeper thinker of the two, wanted to know, 'Are we going to play cricket?'

'Yes, if you want to.' Ben smiled. 'Go and get your bat and ball and the stumps.'

The little boy didn't waste any time. He was back within minutes and they were off, waving their good-byes to James as the car pulled away from Bracken House.

The weather was holding out for them and there wasn't a cloud in the sky. Georgina was determined that there weren't going to be any in *her* sky on this bright Saturday morning.

When they arrived at their destination, Ben looked around him at green lawns, silent statues and fountains in profusion in front of a beautiful old house.

'This is great!' he exclaimed, and turned to the children. 'What do you want to do first?'

'See the animals,' they chorused.

'Right! So that's what we'll do,' he said. 'Afterwards, how about some ice cream before we go on all those exciting things in the play areas?'

'Yes, please!' they said.

'And then can we play cricket?' Jolyon asked quietly.

'Then we will play cricket,' Ben assured him, gently ruffling the solemn little boy's hair.

This was what he'd been denied, Georgina thought, as her heart ached with tenderness. They both had.

As if he'd read her thoughts, Ben said, 'Are you all right, Georgina? Tell me if you're feeling tired, won't you?'

She smiled up at him, and he wanted to take her in arms and tell her how much he loved her, but it was the children's day. He didn't want his emotions running riot to spoil it for them.

They did everything they'd come to do, and when it was time for the picnic that Georgina had set out on a grassy slope behind the gracious house Ben told Jolyon, 'When we've had our lunch we'll play cricket.'

'I'll be the wicket keeper, if you like,' Georgina volunteered.

'Great stuff,' Ben said approvingly. 'Jolyon, you can be one of the opening bats and I'll be the other. Pollyanna can be the bowler.'

'She can't do over-arm throws,' Jolyon whispered in his ear. 'I'll be the bowler and Pollyanna can bat.'

James was waiting at the gate when they arrived home. Grubby, tired and happy, the children couldn't wait to tell their father about their day. He said, 'I can tell they've had a really good time. Are you going to come in for a drink?'

'No, but thank you for the offer,' Georgina told him. 'My feet are aching, but we've had a lovely time too.'

'It's been great,' Ben said. 'Your children are terrific, James. You are very fortunate to have them.'

'Yes, I know,' he said in a low voice as he watched them scamper towards the house after saying their thanks and goodbyes. 'Yet I ache all the time because Julie isn't here with us.'

'Georgina and I can sympathise with you. We know all about the agony of loss, but we are at last coming through it, and the world seems a different place.'

* * *

They were home, and Ben was making tea in her kitchen while Georgina sat with her feet up. When he came in, carrying two steaming mugs, she said, 'That was lovely what you said to James. We *are* coming through it, aren't we?'

'Yes,' he said soberly. 'Since I came here I've been remembering only the good times we had with Jamie.'

'That is how it should be,' she told him. Remembering what James had said about his wife, she said, 'Rightly or wrongly, James has kept the faith.'

'And we didn't because our love wasn't strong enough,' he commented.

She turned away to hide the hurt that his words had caused and then, facing him again, said steadily, 'Maybe so, but we've been given a second chance, haven't we?'

She was giving him another opportunity to say what was really in his mind, but again he didn't take it. Instead, he said, 'If you say so. But it doesn't alter the fact that I drove you away. And *you* let me.'

'I'm sorry we got involved in this sort of a discussion,' she told him as she rose to her feet. 'It has spoilt the last few moments of a lovely day. I'll see you on Monday, Ben.'

'So that's it, is it?' he said dryly. 'It's only half past four and I am dismissed.'

'I'm sure you can find something to do. Why not watch the cricket again? You enjoyed it last time, if I remember rightly.'

'I might just do that,' he replied, 'and when it's over make a day of it by dining at the Hollyhocks.'

And what was that meant to be? Georgina wondered

when he'd gone. A hint about where he could be found later?

She wasn't sure she wanted to take him up on it. He'd put the dampener on her hopes with his disparagement of their past relationship, yet after a rest and a shower she was changing into one of her flowing dresses and preparing to walk the short distance to the Hollyhocks as if Ben was willing her to appear.

He was seated at a table by the window and when he heard Emma greeting her as she came in, he rose to his feet and smiled his welcome as if they'd parted on the best of terms.

As he pulled out a chair for her he said in a low voice, 'I'm sorry about earlier. I don't deserve you.'

'No, you don't,' she agreed, and now it was her turn to smile, 'but I'm here, aren't I?'

'Yes, you are, and I hope it isn't only because you're feeding two,' he teased.

'That *could* be the reason, or it might be because there's nothing on television worth watching. Then again it could be because this child of ours is kicking away inside me in protest at the behaviour of its parents and I thought you ought to know.'

He sighed. 'Not parents...parent. I was the one casting the gloom.'

'So let's change the subject, shall we?' she said lightly. 'Are you going to accompany me the next time I go to see Ian?'

He raised a questioning eyebrow in her direction. 'I thought we'd already agreed on that. Yes, of course I am,' he said decisively.

* * *

Unlike the occasion when they'd dined at the smart new restaurant up on the tops, the night was mild as they walked slowly back to their respective cottages.

As they turned on to the lane a badger ambled in front of them, then disappeared into the darkness. Georgina said, 'The people at the post office feed them every night, and they never fail to turn up.'

He'd only been in the place a matter of weeks yet everything that had happened since he'd arrived was engraved upon his mind. Even the smallest happenings, and the big ones, all about being with Georgina again, would stay with him always, like stars in a dark sky, with the moment when he'd discovered she was pregnant the brightest star of all.

He ached to sleep with her again, to be able to reach out in the darkness and hold the pliant warmth of her in his arms again. And then when daylight came to have breakfast together. Just simple things but for those starved of them precious beyond belief.

Did *she* ever feel like that? he wondered. If she did, she hid it well. She'd made a point of telling him that day at the hospital. How she was her own woman and not interested in any of the advances of the opposite sex, and he'd known that it included himself.

It had been a blow to the heart, but even worse had been the knowledge that *he* was to blame for it, and it could be that any warmth she was showing towards him was either out of pity or put on just to get the waiting time over until the baby was born.

Georgina was observing his expression and commented, 'I thought we had banished the gloom.'

'We have,' he said firmly, and told himself to be satisfied with what they'd got, instead of wishing for the moon.

He wasn't invited in for a nightcap this time. If he had been he would have accepted, yet it didn't matter. He'd just told himself to think positive and that was what he was going to do. He did that in every other aspect of his life, but what there was, or was not, between Georgina and himself was as delicate as gossamer.

As Georgina lay looking up at the night sky through her bedroom window, the day that was past was occupying her thoughts and they were a jumble of pleasure and pain. There'd been the happy hours with the children that had made the longing for a family of her own so bad she could almost taste it.

Then the fall to earth over what Ben had said about the quality of their love in time of need, and last but not least she'd been back up in the clouds as they'd walked home together in the gloaming.

Her spirits had been up and down more times than a yo-yo and in the middle of it all was the longing to be not just the mother of Ben's baby but the cherished wife that she'd once been.

The resident owl hooted to announce its nocturnal presence and taking comfort from that small moment of normality, she slept.

CHAPTER EIGHT

WITH no problems apart from the usual discomforts of pregnancy, Georgina was counting the days to the birth. The baby's head was down in the right position now and when she was called out to the Quarmbys' cottage on Lord Derringham's estate one morning, Christine said on opening the door to her, 'Dr Adams! I wasn't expecting it to be you that came. Shouldn't you be resting?'

'I'm fine, Christine,' she told her laughingly. 'Just a little out of breath and my feet are rather puffy at the end of the day, but that is all. *You* are the one I am concerned about, so tell me what's wrong today, my dear.'

'It isn't me this time,' she explained. 'It's Dennis. He would have come to the surgery as he doesn't like a fuss, but I didn't think he should drive.'

'So what's wrong and where is he?' she asked.

'He's falling about all over the place, can't keep his balance. The moment he got up this morning it was there. The room was spinning and he couldn't stand up straight. He's gone back to bed.'

'And this is the first time it has happened?'

'Yes, to this extent. He's had a few minor dizzy spells before but they've only lasted a matter of minutes. Today it's much worse.'

'This kind of thing can be due to low blood pressure,' Georgina said when she'd tested it and examined the gamekeeper's eyes and ears, 'but I think not in your case, Mr Quarmby. Have you had any headaches?'

'No, but my ears have been tender and painful,' he mumbled irritably, and she thought that for once Dennis Quarmby wasn't in control and he wasn't liking it.

She nodded. 'Vertigo, which it most likely is, comes from a disturbance of the nerves in the canals in the ears. I'm going to prescribe some antihistamine tablets that will help to restore your balance, and in the meantime you need rest and quiet.'

He groaned. 'And while I'm having that the poachers will be out on the estate in full force if they know that I'm laid low.'

'You should soon be much better once you start taking the medication,' she told him, 'and don't get stressed. If the attacks persist we'll look into it further, but for now just take the tablets and keep calm.'

Dennis Quarmby's glance was on his wife hovering anxiously beside the bed and he said, 'I can't be ill, Doctor. Christine needs me. This vile thing that she's got isn't getting any better and I can't bear to see her suffer so.'

'Hush,' Christine said gently. 'We both know that it isn't going to go away, but we love each other, Dennis, and as long as that never changes, we'll be all right.'

He reached out, took her hand in his, and said gruffly, 'Aye, Chrissie, nothing can take that away from us.'

Driving back down to the village Georgina's thoughts were back there with the Quarmbys. Sjögren's syndrome was an incurable autoimmune disorder related to the rheumatoid arthritis that Christine had been diagnosed with and, as she'd said, it wasn't going to go away. In fact, it could get worse, so the outlook was bleak.

But those two had something more precious than gold in the way they loved each other. She and Ben had been blessed with that kind of love once. Would it blossom again in the last days of spring when their child came into the world?

When she arrived back at the surgery, Ben said, 'You look very solemn. Is everything all right?'

With the Quarmbys still at the forefront of her mind she told him, 'Yes. I suppose so. I've just been with two people who love each other very much.'

'And?'

'It reminded me of how we used to be.'

She saw him flinch and regretted the words as soon as she'd said them.

'Maybe they've never lost a child,' he commented flatly.

Contrite, she reached out to take his hand in hers, but as if he hadn't seen the gesture Ben walked through the main doors of the surgery towards his car. Deflated and upset, Georgina watched him drive off on his own calls.

* * *

David Tremayne had been for an interview with a view to joining the practice at the end of May when his contract at St Gabriel's was up. When he'd gone the three doctors had all expressed their approval of the possible newcomer, having been impressed by his brisk yet friendly manner and his unmistakable enthusiasm for his calling.

In his early thirties and unmarried, he was tall and very attractive, and Georgina thought that a mother somewhere must be proud of her handsome son.

James had asked Ben to sit in on the interview even though he was just a temporary member of the practice, and the more she saw them together the more Georgina was aware that the two men had taken an instant liking to each other.

When the interview was over, she had carried on for the rest of the day with an easier mind regarding her own arrangements and that evening when Ben arrived home from the surgery, he came to have a chat about the day's events.

'So what do you think about David Tremayne?' he asked.

'He seemed a really nice guy,' she replied, 'but it's how good a doctor he is that matters most. I do hope that he can join us when he's free, but first James and Elaine will have to sort out the admin side of it.'

The next subject was her appointment with the gynaecologist the following day. 'I'll meet you at his rooms, as I did the last time,' he said. 'Just in case I'm on the last minute getting away from surgery. I presume you're taking the afternoon off as you did before? Have you any concerns to discuss with him?'

'No. Not really. I keep getting a touch of indigestion, which I suppose is because the baby is pressing on my digestive tract, but apart from that I'm all right.'

'Blood pressure still behaving itself?'

'Yes. I seem to have escaped that problem this time.'

'Good.'

She made tea for them, and he perched himself on a kitchen stool while he drank it. He'd been cooler since she'd mentioned the Quarmbys to him, still caring but withdrawn, while she was aching for love and tenderness.

Ben's thoughts on the matter were that what she'd said had been a veiled reproach and he'd thought grimly that no one regretted what had happened to their marriage more than him, but at least he was trying to make up for it.

Georgina was early for the appointment with Ian Sefton and as she sat in the empty waiting room, leafing through a magazine while she waited for Ben, the man she was waiting to see came through on his way back from one of his clinics at the hospital. When he saw her, he stopped for a quick chat.

'Hi, Georgina,' he said. 'Did Ben tell you I phoned the other night to suggest we might meet up to discuss our work? I didn't realise that you and Ben Allardyce were a couple until he joined you at your last appointment.'

'There didn't seem any need to mention it,' she

replied, playing it down. 'We've only just renewed our acquaintance.'

'Yes, he told me. Ben said that you'd been apart, but were together again now and starting this new family.' Moving towards his consulting room, he said good-naturedly, 'I'll be ready for you as soon as he arrives. While I'm waiting I'm going to have a quick cuppa. Those clinics can be gruelling places.'

So Ben had told him that they were together again, she thought. But that wasn't strictly true. So why had he said it? To impress? She didn't think so. That wasn't his style.

As soon as Ben arrived, the receptionist smiled across at them, and said, 'Mr Sefton is ready for you, if you'd like to go in.'

'So, any changes or problems?' Ian asked as he examined her.

'I'm experiencing Braxton Hicks contractions more often,' she told him, 'which I know is normal, so I'm not going to mistake them for labour pains. They're too far apart, for one thing.'

'Yes, they're spaced-out contractions of the uterus and become more noticeable as pregnancy progresses,' he replied.

'And my blood pressure was up this morning. Not all that much but when I checked, it was up.'

She was aware of Ben tensing beside her but avoided his concerned expression as the gynaecologist said, 'Ah, now, that is a different matter. Where the Braxton Hicks are no cause for concern, hypertension most certainly is. So let's see what is going on with that.'

When he tested it for himself he said, 'Yes, it's up, though as you said not a lot. Nevertheless, it's going to mean resting to get it down. At this stage we can't take any chances, Georgina, as I'm sure I don't need to tell you.' He turned to Ben. 'Take the lady home and put her to bed for a couple of days and we'll see how the hypertension is then.'

She groaned. 'I'm needed at the practice.'

'We'll manage without you,' Ben told her levelly. 'You and the baby come first.'

'I do know that,' she told him in chilly tones. The idea of him giving Ian Sefton the impression that all was well with their relationship was still niggling at her.

When they left the building, Ben said, 'Why the drop in temperature?'

'There isn't one. I was just a bit taken aback when Ian Sefton said that you'd told him we were together again.'

'What did you expect me to say? That the baby is a mistake, that we're playing cat and mouse with each other all the time? It was easier to pretend that all was well between us. So, why didn't you mention your blood pressure while we were at the surgery this morning?'

'Because I had the appointment this afternoon. I would have told you about it if I hadn't, but there didn't seem any reason to alarm you at that stage.'

'And at what stage would you have thought it necessary if we hadn't been coming here?'

'Look, Ben,' she said wearily. 'I'm doing what I've

been told and am going home to bed, so calm down. Nothing is going to happen to this baby.'

'And what about something happening to *you*?' he called after her retreating figure, but there was no reply. Georgina was already in her car and pulling away from the forecourt of the building, leaving him with no alternative but to return to his patients.

As she drove back to Willowmere Georgina's annoyance was draining away. How could she have belittled Ben's consideration for her by not telling Ian Sefton the full story? She should be grateful that he cared. He'd lost a child and he would have been living with the thought that there would never be another. Why should he feel that he had to spell out what was happening in their lives to a stranger? She was getting to be a bit prickly. Dared she blame it on hormones?

Their heated exchange of words had put their relationship on an even more shaky footing, and as she pulled up in front of her cottage she was wondering where they went from here.

She rang James on the bedside phone once she was settled against the pillows and, as she'd known he would be, he was totally supportive. 'We will cope all right here,' he assured her. 'Ben is a tower of strength, and if it isn't possible for you to come back before the baby comes, we have David Tremayne joining us towards the end of May. So you will be free to return whenever you feel ready once you have the baby.'

When she'd put the phone down Georgina turned her head into the pillow and wept. She wanted this baby just

as much as Ben did, but its coming would be marred if
she and he had separate lives.

She'd put a key through his letterbox before going into
her own place so that he could let himself in if he
wanted to. Sure enough, seconds after he'd arrived
home early that evening he was bounding up the stairs
and knocking on her bedroom door. That nearly brought
the tears back. The only man she'd ever slept with having to wait to be invited into her bedroom.

'Have you eaten?' were his first words when she
called for him to come in, and that made her smile the
tears away. He'd obviously put their earlier crossing of
swords to one side and was about to take on the role of
head nurse.

She shook her head. 'I wasn't hungry when I got
home but I'm peckish now.'

'So shall I go and raid the larder?'

'Yes, if you like, though anything will do, Ben, just
a slice of toast or whatever. But make something sub-
stantial for yourself while you're there.'

Twenty minutes later he appeared with a tray on
which was an omelette and a soft roll, tea in a china cup,
and a small vase with just one early rose in it. As she
raised herself up off the pillows she said softly, 'Not so
long ago you said you did not deserve me. It is the
other way round, I think. I'm sorry for what I said
earlier. Can you forgive me?'

He placed the tray on the bedside table and replied
with a quizzical smile that gave no hint of anything
other than light-heartedness, 'Yes, if you promise to eat

every crumb. Before I go back downstairs, what about dessert? I've brought some fresh fruit in with me and some ice cream, and I caught the Hollyhocks on the point of closing and coaxed a couple of cream cakes from Emma.'

'I'd like a cream cake. Let's save the fruit and ice cream for tomorrow. Now, will you please go and have *your* meal? You must be starving.'

He was, Ben thought as he went downstairs, but it was the love they'd once had that he was hungry for. Tarnished and neglected, it hadn't disappeared during the lonely years. It was still there if only they could forget past hurts and walk into the light together with a new brother or sister to Jamie.

His nerves had knotted when Georgina had announced that her blood pressure was up, and once they'd eaten, another check would be a good idea.

He was going to suggest he stay the night and was expecting her to protest that it wasn't necessary, but he wasn't going to take no for an answer. The baby was due very soon and it was vital that he should be there for her now…and afterwards.

When he went back upstairs Georgina was asleep, her dark mane splayed across the pillow and her breathing regular enough, considering the weight she was carrying. He'd brought the cream cake with him and placed it on the bedside table when he'd removed the empty tray.

As he kissed her gently on the brow she stirred in her sleep and murmured his name, and in that moment he thought tenderly that she had been keen to make it clear that she was her own woman, but as she'd said his name it had been as if once more she was *his* woman, and for that to be so was all he would ever ask.

While she was sleeping he went next door to collect his things for the night ahead, and when he got back she was awake, face flushed with sleep, eyelids drooping and about to check her blood pressure.

'I'll do that,' he said gently, and when it was done, he was smiling. 'It's normal,' he announced. 'It must have just been a blip, but we do need to keep a close watch on it.'

'So can I get up, Doctor?' she teased, as relief washed over her.

'No. I'm afraid not,' he replied in a similar manner. 'Maybe tomorrow, but for now stop where you are. I intend to stay the night and no protests, please.'

'All right,' she agreed meekly.

'How would you feel if I moved in after the baby is born?' he said, but she shook her head.

'I don't know, Ben,' she said awkwardly, 'let's wait and see.'

'I would be in the spare room—as I will be tonight,' he commented dryly.

'Yes, I know,' she said lamely. 'But if you hadn't come to Willowmere I would have had to cope alone, and I've got used to doing that.'

'All right,' he said levelly. 'Just be sure you don't put the baby at risk with your independence.' On that word of warning, he turned and went downstairs.

He came back up again some time later, to make up

the spare bed and to bring her some supper, but that was the last she saw of him as the night closed in upon them.

The next morning she went downstairs and found Ben making the breakfast. Before he asked, she told him that her blood pressure was normal.

'Good,' he said with a tight smile, and placed bacon and eggs in front of her.

'Your're angry with me, aren't you?' she said in a low voice. 'I know I deserve it. It must seem as if I'm throwing all your kindness back in your face, but it isn't like that, Ben. I'm confused and apprehensive about the future, and I suppose you are the same.'

'Not at all,' he replied. 'The future will take care of itself. I have to be off, Georgina. The surgery opens in ten minutes.'

She'd spoken to the gynaecologist in the middle of the morning and told him that her blood pressure was back to normal and he'd warned her to take care as it could happen again and he wanted to see her again the following week. In the meantime, if she wanted to go back to work there was no reason why not, but to do fewer hours and not overtire herself.

So after another day of rest Georgina had presented herself at the practice once more, free of the anxiety that the minor scare had caused, and had suggested to James that she work afternoons only until the baby was born.

He had agreed immediately and Ben, who had now moved back into his own cottage, watched over her from the sidelines.

Maggie Timmins had given birth to a baby girl earlier in the week, and she was doing well. Every morning when he delivered the milk Bryan had an update on mother and baby to relate.

'What does Josh have to say about his new baby sister?' Georgina had asked when he'd first come with the news.

'He was disappointed at first,' his father said, 'but now that he's adjusted to it he'll sit with her for hours.'

'Have you chosen a name?' she'd enquired.

'Yes,' he replied promptly. 'Rhianna.'

'That's lovely. And Maggie, how is she?'

'Rather nervous after all this time, and we can't wait to bring her home, but doing fine otherwise.'

As Bryan had driven off, Ben's door had opened, and he'd asked, 'Was that the happy father?'

'Yes,' she'd told him. 'It will be your turn soon.'

He'd nodded, for once having no reply, because he was aware that in everything else in his life he was a positive thinker, but when it came to Georgina and the baby he was like a nervous jellyfish.

He knew the reason, of course. Ever since they'd lost Jamie he'd found it impossible to take anything for granted, which had its advantages in his work, but not in his private life.

Georgina had managed without him for three years. She was one of Willowmere's full-time, permanent GPs and extremely capable into the bargain. He knew that she wanted him to be near for their child when it came, but he wasn't getting the impression that it was going to be by her side and in her bed with his wedding ring on her finger.

In the days that followed April showers and spring sunshine were constant reminders of the time of year, and as the calendar moved slowly towards an event that was always celebrated in Willowmere on the first of May, Georgina found herself facing Clare, the owner of the picture gallery, at the other side of her desk.

The two were good friends, and Georgina had been very supportive when Clare had been diagnosed with ovarian cancer some months ago. The smart, middle-aged woman had been operated on to remove the affected organs and was now at the end of a course of chemotherapy and back into organising village affairs once more, something she excelled in.

When she saw her friend seated opposite, Georgina hoped that Clare's presence at the surgery didn't mean any further complications with regard to her health.

It seemed as if that was not the case as her first words were, 'I've come to ask a favour of you, Georgina.'

'Really?' she questioned. 'What is it?'

'The May Day committee has asked me to approach you.'

'Whatever for?'

'They want to know if you will crown the May Queen.'

'Clare, I would love to,' she said regretfully, 'but the baby will be due any day then and I wouldn't want to let them down.'

'We appreciate that, but if you couldn't be there, I would act as stand-in for you. You've only been resident in the village a short time compared to some of us, but you are liked and respected, so please say you will.'

'Yes, of course I will,' she said immediately. 'Pollyanna, James's daughter, has been telling me that she's one of the attendants, and I believe that the Quarmbys' teenage daughter is to be the May Queen, which is good. Christine needs some brightness in her life, but she isn't well enough to be involved actively with her daughter's dress and such.'

'That's under control,' Clare assured her. 'You'll never guess who's offered to make the dress and train…my mother. She's been a gem since I've been ill. I was dreading what she would be like, as Mum can be a tartar over little things, but she's supported me all the time and it's made the cancer problem a lot easier to cope with.'

'That's wonderful,' Georgina said softly. 'When Ben and I lost our son almost four years ago, we had no parents to turn to. Mine died within a short time of each other just before he and I were married, and his were killed in a pile-up on the motorway. So, "tartar" or not, you must cherish her.'

The crowning of the May Queen was an ancient tradition still practised in many English country villages and rural areas to celebrate the coming of summer, a teenage girl being selected to be the Queen and younger ones chosen to be her attendants.

A maypole decked with flowers and with ribbons hanging from it would be erected in the centre of the village green where the crowning ceremony would take place, and once it was over children would dance around the maypole each holding a ribbon.

It was always a special occasion in Willowmere and Georgina thought that Ben would want to watch the proceedings. He was becoming more attracted to village life with each passing day, and whatever they ended up doing in the future he would want their baby to be brought up in the fresh air and friendliness of the countryside.

What he would say when he discovered she'd accepted the honour that the folks of Willowmere were anxious to bestow upon her she didn't know, but if she was mobile and not in the labour ward at St Gabriel's, she would perform it with the greatest of pleasure.

When she told him he smiled and said, 'It is a nice thought but—'

'I know,' she interrupted. 'You were going to say I might be occupied elsewhere. I've cleared that with Clare. She will perform the crowning ceremony if I can't be there.' She paused and smiled. 'I'm glad this child of ours will be a spring baby.'

'Why especially?'

'It was spring when you came back into my life, when daffodils were nodding in cottage gardens and there were newborn lambs in the fields.'

Surely he would understand the message in what she'd just said, Georgina thought, and take her up on it, but he just smiled a wry smile and carried on trimming the hedge around his garden.

So much for that, she thought. Was Ben still of the opinion that in spite of the closeness of their lives in recent weeks, it still wasn't working? Had he actually been into the estate agent's to see what properties were for sale in the village? She hoped not.

There was one house that had been for sale in recent weeks that she'd always longed to live in. It was a large, detached property, built out of local limestone, and it stood among the green fields of Cheshire.

She'd always thought what an attractive house it was, though not the kind of residence for a single mother, and she wouldn't have been able to afford it in any case if it had ever come up for sale, but it was on the market now and no doubt would soon be snatched up by someone with an eye for solid elegance.

When she'd seen the photograph of it in the estate agent's window, she'd gazed at it enviously and hoped that it wouldn't be bought by someone who would start pulling it apart. Obviously it wasn't going to appeal to Ben. He'd lived alone in the house in London for three years and that was a delightful place, but from what he'd said it may as well have been a stable for all the pleasure he'd derived from living there without his wife and son.

So she couldn't see him getting an urge to buy The Meadows, as the house was called, while he had the up-keep of a large property in London to contend with. And it was like he'd said, they needed somewhere close by when they went to visit the grave so that Jamie would never feel they had deserted him, and the London house would always be somewhere for his brother, Nicholas, to stay if he had business in the capital when he came to the U.K.

It was early morning. As he handed the solicitor next door to the estate agent's a cheque for the deposit on the purchase of the only house that had caught his imagination in Willowmere, Ben was telling himself that he was crazy to be thinking of buying a house as big as The Meadows.

If Georgina didn't want to stand beside him in front of the altar in the village church and repeat the vows they'd once made in the uncomplicated life that had been wrenched out of their grasp, he was going to find himself rattling around the place like a lost soul.

But the moment the estate agent had shown him a photograph of The Meadows he'd asked to view it, and after that he hadn't been able to get it out of his mind. Incredibly it was standing empty and there was no chain involved in the sale so it would soon be his, or theirs if he should be so lucky.

Sometimes he thought Georgina still loved him, but on other occasions, he wasn't at all sure. Maybe when he told her he'd bought The Meadows, he would have a clearer picture of her feelings. If she expressed concern about them still having the London house, he would tell her the good news regarding that.

The last time he'd spoken to Nicholas he'd said that he was considering buying a property in the capital as in the future he would be spending six months in every year there. When he'd suggested that he buy theirs,

Nicholas had jumped at the chance, delighted to become the new owner of the house in the tree-lined square.

It would mean that the loving bonds they still had with their son would remain unbroken because his favourite uncle, who was someone else that Jamie had loved and who had loved him, would be close by for him and for them when either together or apart they brought the white roses of remembrance.

CHAPTER NINE

To Ben's relief Georgina was still asleep when he arrived back at the cottage. He didn't want her to know anything about the house until the baby was born. That way she wouldn't feel that he was forcing the issue of their future relationship in any way.

He didn't know if she was aware that The Meadows was for sale, or even if she knew there was such a place. But she would one day soon and he would be able to tell from her reaction whether he'd made a big mistake in buying one of the most attractive houses in the neighbourhood.

He'd asked the estate agent not to reveal any details of his purchase to anyone, especially his ex-wife, and so far it was all going to plan. Surveys had been satisfactory and he'd got a completion date for the first of May.

He wasn't to know that she hadn't been asleep all the time he'd been absent. She'd heard his door close down below when he was setting off, and had gone to the window and watched him walk down the lane with his familiar purposeful stride, thinking how much she loved him still.

She'd presumed he'd gone to buy a morning paper, so had gone back to bed and dozed off again, but when eventually she surfaced he was puttering around the garden. When she'd showered and dressed, she went down and asked Ben where he'd been. For a moment he looked taken aback. Then he rallied and said he'd been for a walk, which was easy enough to believe on a bright April morning.

Once a month there was a farmers' market in the village hall that was always well attended by local people and others from outlying areas, eager to buy fresh free-range eggs, farmhouse cheeses, and bacon and hams from the pig farms, to name just a few of the whole-some foods on display.

There was also a café at the back of the hall where the husband-and-wife team from the Hollyhocks served snack meals. Altogether it was an occasion not to be missed.

As she was finishing a leisurely breakfast, Ben appeared and suggested that they walk to Willow Lake for exercise, which Georgina thought was odd as he'd already been out doing that same thing. But the suggestion was appealing and when they arrived, they found that the trees from which it had got its name were now bedecked with the new growth that spring brought as they hung over its still waters.

As she looked around her Georgina was remembering Anna and Glenn, now far away in Africa, and how he had proposed to her at this very spot. Would there be a second time round for her and Ben? she wondered. And if there was, would it be for the right reasons?

He was observing her questioningly and, putting to one side wistful thoughts, she said, 'How about we go to do a big shop? There is a farmers' market in the village hall today, the first one since you arrived in Willowmere. When you see what is on sale you'll understand what I mean by a "big shop".'

He was smiling, 'Lead on, then, and surprise me still further with your country customs.'

With a sudden drop in spirits Georgina thought that they were on each other's wavelength in all but one thing…they didn't sleep in the same bed.

There were so many times in the night when the child inside her moved and she longed for Ben to be there to share the special moment of tenderness and joy, but she thought sombrely it would be breaking the rules that they seemed to be living by. He seemed contented enough in his role of onlooker, which made her think all the more that he'd given up on them making their wedding vows for a second time.

As they moved from stall to stall, with Ben carrying their purchases in a large hessian bag that Georgina had brought with her, they were stopped frequently by patients and friends that she'd made during her years in Willowmere. All of them were ready to welcome Ben into their midst, in spite of the curiosity of some who would have liked to know where Dr Adams had been hiding the man by her side.

As they were turning into Partridge Lane on the way home, a luxurious car passed them with a chauffeur at the wheel, and the man on the backseat smiled and waved.

'Who was *that*? Ben exclaimed.

'Lord Derringham,' she told him laughingly. 'He owns an estate up on the tops. Dennis Quarmby is his gamekeeper.'

'I wouldn't expect that you see *him* at the surgery very often,' he commented dryly.

'No. He has private medical care, but I was called out to his wife a few times last year when she was pregnant and was having some problems. He's a decent sort and well liked amongst those who live in the area. Needless to say, he has a very impressive residence that puts every other house for miles around in the shade.'

The comment brought The Meadows to mind and he wondered what she would think when she saw it. There had been a tricky moment earlier when one of the stall-holders had asked Georgina if she was aware that it had been sold and she'd enquired without much show of interest if the farmer's wife knew who'd bought it.

'No, I don't,' had been the reply, 'but there's a rumour going around that it isn't anyone local, and everyone thinks it's a shame.'

On Monday evening Ben came knocking on her door. 'I answered the phone to David Tremayne this morning. He wanted to speak to James, and he and I had a brief conversation. He's still keen to join the practice and is hoping that there will be some definite news on his appointment soon.'

'James and Elaine were discussing it this morning,' she told him. 'It would seem that it's all going ahead satisfactorily, but I can understand that he's anxious to get things sorted.'

'Which makes two of us,' he commented with an edge to his voice.

'What do you mean?' she asked, startled by his tone.

'I would have thought it was obvious. His coming means you can take as long as you want away from the surgery after the birth, but so far your plans, if you have any, seem to be a closely guarded secret.'

'You make it sound so simple,' she said heatedly. 'But it isn't and well you know it!' Before she could say anything she might regret, she grabbed a jacket off the hall stand and marched off down the drive.

He groaned as he watched her go. It was unfor- givable to take out his irritations on Georgina, but he was keen to know what direction their relationship was going in. So far a blissful reconciliation seemed as remote as the silver moon that had appeared on the heels of a glorious sunset.

Until tonight he'd been determined that there would be no persuasion from him. Georgina had to be sure that she really wanted him if they ever got back together, that it wasn't because of the baby but because she still loved him. And so what had he done? Tackled her about it in a manner that had sounded more like bullying than concern.

The only thing to do was to go and find her, bring her home and apologise, even though what she'd said before she'd rushed off had made him feel that he was still not forgiven.

When he went out into the lane, there was no sign of her, and he hesitated. The lake wasn't far away, had she gone there to calm down? He hoped not. It could be unsafe out there in the dark, and suppose she started labour while she was alone?

He was moving in that direction with a fast stride even as he thought it, but there was no one there when he arrived, just the lake and the trees bowing over it.

The village centre was just the opposite when he got there, with the Pheasant as the focal point. It was a mild night and the tables outside were fully occupied. From the buzz of noise issuing from inside it seemed as if it was the same in both parts, but Georgina wasn't amongst the throng.

Gillian Jarvis, the new nurse at the practice, was there with her husband, and when she saw him in the doorway, she came across and asked if he was looking for Georgina. 'We saw her going into the surgery as we drove past,' she said.

With a brief word of thanks, Ben turned on his heel and set off in the direction of the limestone building beside the village green and, sure enough, the lights were on inside when he got there.

He called out as he went in so as not to alarm her and found her sitting in the swivel chair behind her desk, staring into space. She turned at his approach and observed him unsmilingly. Reaching out, he took her hand and lifted her carefully to her feet. When they were facing each other he said gently, 'I'm sorry I took my bad temper out on you, of all people, Georgina.'

The dark hazel eyes looking into his were mirroring

the pain inside her as she told him, 'I behaved no better, Ben. I'm sorry, too. Let's go home.'

'Yes, let's,' he agreed, wanting to hold her close and tell her how much he loved her, yet wary of doing so in case it pushed their relationship further back than it was already.

As they walked the short distance home Georgina said regretfully, 'Have you eaten since you came home from the surgery?'

He shrugged. 'You know me—first things first. I had something on the stove but left it to tell you about David Tremayne. I was keen to see your reaction.'

'You turned the hotplate off, I hope?' she said, as she thought that he'd certainly got her reaction, and it hadn't gone down too well. Her face softened. It hadn't stopped him from coming to look for her, though.

They separated at her door. Ben returned to his cooking and Georgina sat gazing into space as the future that was so hazy didn't become any cleaner.

It was there again, the feeling deep down inside her that, though Ben was thoughtful and caring, it was the baby who held his heartstrings, and could she blame him if that was the case after what they'd lost that day in the park?

She went upstairs to bed as the light was fading and willed herself to blot out everything except the child that was moving inside her. Soon her doubts and dilemmas were submerged in sleep.

Next door, Ben was also deep in thought and he wished they were happier issues that crowded his mind. These should be joyful days for them both, he told himself. Full of excitement and anticipation. If they had a normal relationship, they would be, but neither of them were prepared to make the first move because they didn't want to be hurt again.

It was Friday evening at the end of a week that had passed slowly and uneventfully for the two doctors. They'd each had their evening meal and were seated in the small gardens at the back of the cottages, watching the sun set. When Ben looked across at her, Georgina was staring straight ahead as if she was seeing something that he couldn't see, and out of the blue she said, 'It could be some time before we're able to visit the grave once the baby arrives. Let's go tomorrow.'

Ben was frowning. 'I don't think so. It's a long drive for you in your present state. Why don't I go on my own?'

She was shaking her head emphatically. 'No, I have to go. Something is telling me that I must.'

'What do you mean?' he said slowly. 'Do you feel that the baby might be early so you don't want to leave it any later? If that's the case, it could be risky. I'm quite capable of delivering my own child, but I'm not too keen on having to do it on the motorway or in some other most unsuitable surroundings.'

'I *have* to go,' she insisted.

He sighed. 'What has brought this on? If it means so much, yes, we'll go. We can pick up the flowers on the way. But I don't understand the sudden urgency.'

She was calming down now that he'd agreed and said in a placatory manner, 'The next time we go Jamie will have a new sister or brother. On this occasion I want it to be just the two of us…and him.'

'Fair enough, but I insist we go to the house while we're there so that you can have a rest before we set off back.'

She didn't reply and he knew she was remembering the last time they'd both been there. How it had set off an incredible chain of events that would soon be bearing fruit in the gift of another child, and he still didn't know if that would be the limit of it.

A far as he was concerned, her suggestion had come out of nowhere. He'd been taking it for granted that they would be staying close to base during the last days before the birth and suddenly they were embarking upon a long and tiring journey. It was a fact that pregnant women sometimes behaved out of character due to hormone changes and he supposed that today's sudden urgency fell into that category.

He wasn't to know that for Georgina there were no such misgivings. There had just been an overwhelming urge in her to do what she'd been doing for all the years she'd been apart from Ben. Yet she didn't blame him if he was upset at the way she was making light of his anxieties on behalf of the baby and herself.

They were up early the next morning and while Ben was at the local garage, filling up the tank with petrol, Georgina checked her blood pressure. It was steady, with no increase to concern herself about, and she breathed a sigh of relief, knowing that if it had been up, Ben would have dug his heels in and refused to go, and it would have been common sense to agree.

As if he'd read her mind his first words when he came back were concerning it, and when she'd reassured him, he looked happier about what they were doing, though still unsure of the wisdom of it.

The miles were speeding past and all the time Georgina sat quietly in the passenger seat, speaking only rarely, but each time he looked at her she had a smile for him, and Ben thought that it was going to be the first time they'd visited the grave together, except for the day when he'd found her there and both their lives had changed for ever. Maybe her tranquillity was a way of telling him that it was going to all come right for them?

They'd stopped off in the town to buy the white roses before going onto the motorway and had recently stopped again for an early lunch before they hit the London traffic. As the capital city drew nearer Georgina could feel a strange kind of peace stealing over her. As if all the anxieties and frustrations of past weeks and years were leaving her. She'd seen it in the sunset, the promise of happiness, yet didn't understand how the sad thing they had come all this way for could bring that about.

They'd held hands as they'd placed the flowers on the white marble, united for the first time in a bond of love for their son from which grief had been wiped away, and when they'd said their goodbyes to him and walked back to the car they'd still been holding hands as if neither of them wanted to let go.

When Ben had suggested that they go to the house

so that she might rest for a while, Georgina had agreed without hesitation, and this time she hadn't slumped into his arms, caught up in the in the trauma of a painful return to the place that had once been her home.

Instead, she'd walked around the familiar rooms before letting Ben tuck her up on the sofa for an hour, and as he'd watched over her his thoughts had gone to Nicholas who would soon be living there with maybe children of his own one day.

Whether he and Georgina would ever live together in The Meadows was another matter, but for the moment he was going to put those thoughts to one side.

When it was time to leave, he asked, 'Are you content now that you've been to the cemetery?'

'Yes,' she told him gravely. 'Today it was how it should be for him, the two of us together. The longing to be here came over me suddenly and everything else seemed far away. The birth being so near, the thought of visiting the house again, the long drive, all seemed blurred. All I wanted was come to where we were once so happy.'

'And do you think we will ever be that happy again?' he asked as he helped her into the car.

'Maybe not,' she said softly, still with peace upon her. 'How it was before could be a hard act to follow, but today we've made a move in the right direction, haven't we?' And as the car pulled out of the square she closed her eyes and slept.

She woke up when Ben pulled in at a service stop on the motorway not far from home, and as she observed him questioningly he said, 'I think I might have a flat tyre. Do you want to stretch your legs and have a wander around inside? I'll come and join you as soon as I've changed it.'

Georgina nodded. 'Yes, I'm stiff all over. I'll wait for you outside the restaurant. We may as well eat here to save cooking when we get back.' And left him to sort out the tyre.

It was a big place. There were shops of various kinds along the passage that led to the restaurant on the first floor and, considering the time of day, there weren't many people about.

After pottering around for a while she lowered herself onto the seating outside a toy shop next to the restaurant and positioned herself where she could see Ben when he came in at the main entrance below.

As she glanced around her she saw a young family approaching. Mother, father, with a small boy of a similar age and colouring to how Jamie had been and just as fast in his movements. He was running on in front, watched dotingly by his parents, and as she smiled at him he stopped abruptly beside her.

When Georgina glanced to see what had caught his attention, she saw that it was the wooden display case next to where she was sitting. Inside it were some of the toys sold in the shop.

It was glass fronted and locked and after hesitating for a moment, the boy reached out and pulled at the handle to get to the toys. As he did so, the whole thing began to topple towards him.

She heard his mother scream and his father's footsteps pounding on the tiled floor as she heaved herself towards him and dragged him out of the way. And then there was nothing but pain and darkness.

Ben was smiling as he came through the main door. They would be home safe and sound in minutes. There had been no need for him to fuss like he had. It had been a wonderful day with those special tranquil moments with their son followed by that quiet time in the home they'd once shared, and all the time he'd been able to feel Georgina's contentment around him in unspoken promises.

When they were back home, he was going to ask her to marry him again. He should have done it before, instead of being so set on waiting until he saw how things were when the baby came. That was how it ought to be, making their vows to each other once more as a separate thing that wasn't tied in with anything else except their love for each other. And if he was taking too much for granted after this wonderful day together, at least Georgina would know how much he still adored her.

As he stepped onto the escalator he heard a crash and someone screamed above, then a voice bellowed, 'Phone for an ambulance and tell them the lady's pregnant, due any time by the looks of it!' As his happy bubble burst around him Ben was leaping up the moving staircase in sick dismay, praying that it wasn't Georgina who was being described, yet knowing it would be too big a coincidence if it wasn't.

At the worst he was expecting to find that she'd gone into premature labour, but it was worse than that, much worse. She was lying very still on her side, curled up in a foetal position with her arms folded protectively across her stomach. Two security men were frantically removing the large wooden display case that she was lying under.

He was by her side in a flash, telling them in a voice as cold as steel, 'I'm her husband and I'm a doctor. Tell me what happened.'

There was a woman weeping silently just a foot away and she said chokingly, 'Your wife saved our little boy. He'd seen the toys inside and was pulling at the handle. She saw what was about to happen and dragged him away as it started to fall, but didn't have time to protect herself. We are so sorry.'

Not as much as I am, he thought grimly as he registered a faint pulse and shallow breathing. He was shuddering to think what might have happened to the baby. But for the moment she was his main concern. He could see a deep gash on the side of her head and her legs were bleeding from cuts that the glass in the doors of the display unit had made when they had shattered. Any other injuries would not be immediately visible until she was examined in Accident and Emergency at St Gabriel's, which was the nearest hospital as they were so close to home.

The ambulance had been mercifully quick and after they'd taken Georgina down in the lift on a stretcher they were soon away with sirens blaring.

Ben had caught a glimpse of the child who'd innocently been the cause of the accident clinging to his mother's hand, and with a pang thought how much like

Jamie he was. Had this been another reason why Georgina had felt impelled to leave the safety of Willowmere? he'd thought incredulously. And now that they'd made peace at their son's grave was he going to lose her?

Ian Sefton was waiting for them when the stretcher was wheeled into A and E with Ben granite-faced beside it, and he said, 'We've got a team standing by for Georgina but first I'm going to check the baby's heartbeat on the foetal monitor to make sure it's OK.' It was with great relief he announced, 'We have a heartbeat. That's the good news. But it's not quite as strong as I would like it to be.'

Ben nodded with hope hard to come by as he gazed at Georgina still and bloodstained on the bed.

'I'll be standing by in case I have to do a Caesarean section,' the gynaecologist said, and Ben thought that was how he would be if it was someone else's wife and child, but on this occasion he was on the receiving end and was numb with the horror of what was happening to their hopes and dreams.

He'd had high blood pressure on his mind while Georgina had been carrying the baby because it had happened once before, or had thought that some other medical problem might put her and the baby at risk, but from out of nowhere had come a different kind of danger, horrifying and unexpected.

A child in danger had been something that she hadn't been able to ignore and she was paying the price. Why, oh, why, hadn't he told her how much he loved her before this?

* * *

Severe concussion, broken ribs and deep cuts, especially to the head and legs, were the total of Georgina's injuries, and one of the doctors commented to another that if she hadn't been carrying so much extra weight, it might have been a lot worse.

She still hadn't regained consciousness when she started to haemorrhage, and then it was panic stations with the theatre on standby for the Caesarean section that Ian Sefton had anticipated.

At just past midnight Arran Allardyce came into the world, and Ben wept at the nature of his coming, even though from all appearances he was a lusty infant. His mother, on the other hand, still hadn't surfaced from the accident and the anaesthetic she'd been given during the operation, and was not aware of his arrival. As Ben kept a vigil by her bedside, with the baby sleeping peacefully beside them, he was willing Georgina to come back to them so that he could tell her how much he loved her.

As dawn brightened the night sky Georgina opened her eyes, removed the hand that he'd been holding out of his clasp and passed it slowly over her stomach. Ben saw that her eyes were awash with tears,

'I'm so sorry, Ben,' she said weakly, 'but I had to save the boy. Did you see how much he looked like Jamie?' Tears were rolling down her cheeks now as she begged, 'Can you forgive me for losing another of our children?'

'I can forgive you anything,' he said softly, 'because I love you more than life itself. And what's this about losing the baby? If you turn your head sideways, you will see young Arran Allardyce, strong and healthy despite a slightly early entrance into the world, sleeping peacefully beside you, Georgina, unharmed and totally beautiful, just like his mother.'

Her smile was brighter than the sun that would soon be in the sky as she cried joyfully, 'So Jamie has a brother! How absolutely perfect, and how wonderful that you still love me as much as I love you.

'That day when we were having the picnic and you said that the second chance we'd been given wasn't working, it made me realise just how much I wanted it to, and ever since then I've been afraid to plan a future in which we were together in every sense of the word in case you were right.'

'Will you marry me when you've recovered from all the dreadful things that have happened to you during the last twenty-four hours?' he asked softly.

'Those will be forgotten when I hold our baby in my arms,' she told him, 'and, yes, of course I'll marry you, Ben. I've always felt as if I was still your wife in any case, but now we can start living again, waking up each morning in the same bed, you and I together like it used to be, with Arran close by in the nursery.'

Ian Sefton was approaching and when he reached the bedside, he said whimsically, 'You had us all worried for a while, Georgina. I'd almost decided I would have to emigrate if I let anything happen to you and the baby. This husband of yours was all scrubbed up ready to take over if I put a foot wrong.'

'Were you really?' she asked Ben.

'Yes, I'm afraid so,' he replied. 'There was too much at stake.'

'So, do I get an invitation to the wedding for a job well done?' the gynaecologist asked.

Ben was smiling. 'You do indeed,' he told him, and then added in a more serious manner, 'You were the best, Ian. We can't thank you enough.'

When he'd gone, Ben lifted little Arran carefully out of his crib and placed him in his mother's arms, and as he gazed at them in that special moment it seemed as if it had been a good idea after all to buy The Meadows. There would be no more confusion in their minds regarding the future. They were a family again.

That same evening they were visited by another family, one that might not have been so complete if it hadn't been for Georgina's instinctive reaction at the motorway services.

When the parents and their small son stood beside her bed the young one's father said, 'So what do you say to the lady for saving you from being hurt by the display case, Dominic?'

'Thank you for saving me,' he told her in a voice that indicated he'd been rehearsing the little speech.

'And?' his mother prompted, placing a gift-wrapped parcel in his hands.

'This is for your baby,' he said shyly. 'What are you going to call him?'

'We're going to call him Arran,' she told him gently, 'and I'm sure he will love what is inside this present when he is a bit older.' Then she turned to his parents.

'You didn't have to do this. I'm just so pleased that Dominic wasn't hurt. We lost our first child in an accident and I wouldn't wish that sort of grief on anyone.'

When they'd gone, she asked Ben, 'Were you angry when you knew what I'd done?'

'Horrified, yes, but not angry.' he told her softly. 'It would have been amazing if you hadn't stepped in, being the nearest to him. In those kind of moments there is no time for thinking, do I, or don't I? One just goes ahead and does it.'

CHAPTER TEN

IT WAS an occasion they would long remember when Ben brought Georgina and baby Arran home to the cottage in Partridge Lane and in the hours that followed it was as if the whole village was sharing their happiness.

And there was more to come. Ben still had a couple of pleasant surprises for her but felt they could wait for a day or two. The injuries she'd received from the broken glass were healing satisfactorily and the hospital, as was usually the case, was leaving the fractured ribs to heal of their own accord. But she was still a little weak from the trauma that had followed when Ian Sefton had been forced to do a Caesarean baby to save its life and hers.

Arran was fine. Every time they observed him they rejoiced. Ben was taking time off from work to be there during the first important days of his son's life and so that Georgina could rest as she recovered from the accident and her delivery.

It was an irksome situation when she was raring to be back to her usual fitness but, acknowledging that it was a necessary procedure, she had to be content with welcoming a constant stream of wellwishers from the comfort of the sofa while Ben took charge of everything else.

On the second afternoon of her return Clare was one of the callers and after she'd held the baby reverently and then handed him back to his watchful father she said, 'I know it's pushing it, Georgina, you've only been home a couple of days, but it's the May Queen crowning on Saturday. Would you feel up to doing the ceremony?'

'I'd love to,' she told her. 'I'm feeling stronger all the time and as long as Ben and Arran are there beside me I'll be fine. How are the preparations going?'

'All right so far,' was the reply, 'and now that you're prepared to do the crowning, my last worry is sorted. My mum has finished the dresses, the music is organised and refreshments are in the capable hands of our Hollyhocks friends.'

'And how are you amongst all this activity?' Georgina asked, not overlooking that the woman sitting opposite was coping with a very worrying health problem, as well as the May Queen arrangements.

'Not so bad,' she replied. 'The chemo took it out of me but, as I've said before, my mother gives me lots of support. It has taken something like this to bring us together. I've always been very self-sufficient and capable, and now that I'm sick and apprehensive of what lies ahead, it's bringing out the best in her.'

'*We* have something to ask of *you*, Clare, haven't we, Ben?' Georgina said, and he nodded.

'Will you be Arran's godmother?'

She watched Clare's eyes fill with tears and knew what was coming next.

'I can't think of anything I would love more,' she choked, 'but a godmother needs to be someone there for him long term and I can't promise that, can I, in my present state?'

'I know how much Georgina values you as a friend,' Ben told her, 'and with your courage and spirit, you'll be an inspiration to our son. So do please say yes.'

She was smiling now. 'How can I say anything else after that? Thanks for being so kind. You can count me in.'

The godfather slot had always belonged to Nicholas, and when Ben had rung him from the hospital to say that the baby had arrived and that Georgina was doing as well as could be expected, he'd said, 'Don't give me that hospital jargon, Ben. What do you mean?'

He'd been appalled when Ben had told him the full story, but had perked up when he'd discovered that there was a second role they wanted him to play in their lives, that of best man, and the knowledge that the two people he cared for most were going to remarry had left him on cloud nine.

It was drizzling out of a grey sky when the villagers awoke on Saturday morning and as Georgina gave Arran his first feed of the day, with Ben propped up against the pillows beside her, she wailed, 'I don't believe it. We've had nothing but sunshine for days and just look out there!'

But by the middle of the morning the rain had gone

and blue skies had appeared, with the sun shining extra brightly as if to compensate for its earlier absence, and all was hustle and bustle around the village green.

A wooden platform had been erected at one end, with steps leading up to it for the crowning ceremony, and in the middle of the green was the maypole with its bright ribbons wrapped tightly around it until such time as they were needed.

On the dot of twelve Willowmere's own brass band began to lead the May Day procession around the village with the vicar at the front and the Queen and her attendants walking sedately behind in their pretty long dresses.

They arrived at the village green at exactly twelve o'clock and the first people Georgina saw when she and Ben took their positions on the platform, with Arran cradled safely in his father's arms, were the Quarmbys, with Dennis puffed out with pride as he saw his daughter approach the rostrum and Christine, pale but very happy by his side.

When Georgina looked away from them, Pollyanna was waving from her place in the Queen's retinue, and James, another proud father, wasn't far away from her with Jolyon by his side. But she thought contentedly that the proudest father of all was standing beside her with his son in his arms and all was well with her world.

The crowning of the May Queen and the festivities that had followed it were over and in the early evening Georgina and Ben were pushing the pram homewards when he said, 'That was a great day, but I've got something that could top that or, on the other hand, maybe it won't.'

'What is it?' she asked, eyes bright with curiosity as they walked the last hundred yards to the cottage.

'You'll find out tomorrow, not before,' he said teasingly, with his dark eyes adoring her, and she pulled a face but didn't pursue it.

The sale of The Meadows had been completed a couple of days ago.

He was in possession of the keys to the lovely old house and was eager to see Georgina's reaction, all the time wondering if he should have let her have a say in where they were going to bring up Arran. But at that time he hadn't known what direction they were going in and had faced the fact that he might have to resell it or live there alone.

It was Nicholas offering to buy the London house that had made up his mind for him and he had yet to find out what Georgina would think of *that*.

'So do you want us to walk or drive to where we're going?' he questioned the next morning when they'd finished breakfast and Arran had been fed.

'It depends how far,' she replied.

'It's a mile or so.'

'Then we'll walk. May I ask in what direction?'

'Towards the Timmins farm. Baby Rhianna is home now and thriving.'

She was smiling. 'We're not going on a comparing-babies outing, are we?'

'We can call on them if you like but, no, that isn't where we're going. You'll just have to wait and see.'

The house was aptly named, Ben thought as they walked past fields where sheep and cattle grazed on the greenest grass he'd ever seen, and as they turned a bend on the lane on which it stood it was there, silent and empty, waiting for *them*.

'I wonder who's bought The Meadows,' Georgina said regretfully. 'Maggie Timmins has heard that it's a townie.'

'She's heard right.'

'What do you mean?'

'Well, you can hardly call me a country boy, can you?'

'You!' she cried. 'You, Ben! You've bought The Meadows for us.'

He held out his hand and on the flat of his palm were the keys.

'I hope you're going to like it.'

'Like it!' she whooped, throwing her arms around him. 'I've always loved this house. When, though? How? What made you…?' she gasped excitedly.

'It was when I knew that I couldn't live without you any more.'

Her excitement was lessening. 'But can we afford two houses? What about our house in the square?'

'It's sold.'

'And you never consulted me!'

'I didn't need to. Someone you love is going to live there and we'll be able to visit whenever we want.'

She was bewildered. 'Who?'

'Who is your favourite man...next to me?'

Light was dawning. 'Nicholas?'

'Yes. My young brother wants a house in London and is only too pleased to buy ours, so Jamie won't be all alone there while we're up here. He'll have his uncle Nick close by.'

Her radiance was back as she held him close and told him. 'I can live with that, Ben.'

He jangled the keys in front of her again. 'So now can we go inside?'

'Just try and stop me,' she told him as she picked Arran up out of the pram and cradled him in her arms.

As they walked around the spacious rooms and took in the views from every window Ben was jubilant. They were going to be so happy in this place, he thought. Their son was going to grow up in the beautiful Cheshire countryside in one of the nicest family homes around.

Just a few weeks ago it would have been a dream, now it was a reality, a reality where Georgina still loved him, they had a son, and they were going to live in this gorgeous house.

James had been round to the cottage to see Arran and to discuss Georgina's future role at the surgery and they had come to a decision that she was going to take the full maternity leave and then would return part time if a suitable arrangement could be made regarding Arran's care during those hours.

In the meantime, it would leave James and David Tremayne as full-time doctors, and Ben would be able to go back to paediatrics.

* * *

When Edwina Crabtree, bellringer in chief, heard that there was to be a wedding in the village very soon and that the two participants were Dr Adams and the ex-husband she'd produced from nowhere, she nodded approvingly. They now had a child and if there was one thing that Edwina liked to see it was all loose ends tied up neatly.

In her own staid way she liked Georgina Adams—soon to be Allardyceonce more. Dr Adams was always kind and tactful when she was forced to consult her and in honour of the occasion, she was going to see that the bells pealed out across Willowmere on her wedding day more joyously than they'd ever done before.

An invitation to the wedding reception at The Meadows had mellowed Edwina even more until she discovered that she wasn't the only one to receive such a thing, that half the village had been invited.

Unaware of the prim campanologist's good feelings towards them, Georgina and Ben were making their preparations for a second taking of their marriage vows.

Pollyanna was to be the only bridesmaid and was being quite blasé about the occasion, saying that she didn't want pink again as it was what she'd worn as a bridesmaid not so long ago to her aunt Anna, now far away in Africa. So a pretty dress of pale green had been produced and she was delighted.

Nicholas was due any time from Texas to do the double act of best man and godfather at Arran's christening, which was to take place shortly before the wedding, and when she heard about that arrangement, Edwina was positively beaming.

For Georgina and Ben the days were filled with tenderness and contentment and it was all going to come together in the village church, the two ceremonies that would set the seal on the future that they'd thought they would never have.

The christening was in the morning and the wedding was in the afternoon. Those present were just Clare and Nicholas, as godparents, and Georgina and Ben in the church that was decked out with flowers for the wedding later.

As they each made their vows with regard to the tiny child in his godmother's arms there was a feeling of timelessness around them in the old stone church, of baptisms, weddings and funerals, some recent, others long gone.

When the vicar took the baby from Clare, dipped his fingers into the baptismal font and christened him Arran Benjamin, there were tears on his mother's lashes.

On seeing them, his father took her hand in his and held it tightly because he knew from where they came. They had another son, absent but cherished beyond belief, and one day they would tell Arran about his brother.

The moment had passed. The baptism was over and Arran was back in his mother's arms as they made their way outside and proceeded to Georgina's cottage where the four of them would remain until it was time to get dressed for the wedding.

As they ate a snack lunch the church bells were pealing triumphantly across Willowmere and Ben said, 'Surely that can't be for us!'

'I believe it is,' Clare told him. 'Edwina and her friends are in fine fettle today.'

They were going to use the same ring as before, which had never been off Georgina's finger since the occasion when Ben had placed it there. Today it was safely in Nicholas's pocket but would soon be back where it belonged.

When Georgina came slowly down the stairs some time later, beautiful in a calf-length dress of oyster silk that emphasised her dark eyes and hair, she was carrying beautiful flowers from the garden of the house that would soon be their home.

Ben was waiting for her at the bottom step in his own wedding finery and when he opened his arms, she went into them like a ship into harbour… And the wedding bells continued to swing high in the bell tower as they pealed out for two people who had once lost their way and were about to be united in the love that had been mislaid rather than lost.

MILLS & BOON®
Pure reading pleasure™

FEBRUARY 2009 HARDBACK TITLES

ROMANCE

The Spanish Billionaire's Pregnant Wife	Lynne Graham
The Italian's Ruthless Marriage Command	Helen Bianchin
The Brunelli Baby Bargain	Kim Lawrence
The French Tycoon's Pregnant Mistress	Abby Green
Forced Wife, Royal Love-Child	Trish Morey
The Rich Man's Blackmailed Mistress	Robyn Donald
Pregnant with the De Rossi Heir	Maggie Cox
The British Billionaire's Innocent Bride	Susanne James
The Timber Baron's Virgin Bride	Daphne Clair
The Magnate's Marriage Demand	Robyn Grady
Diamond in the Rough	Diana Palmer
Secret Baby, Surprise Parents	Liz Fielding
The Rebel King	Melissa James
Nine-to-Five Bride	Jennie Adams
Marrying the Manhattan Millionaire	Jackie Braun
The Cowboy and the Princess	Myrna Mackenzie
The Midwife and the Single Dad	Gill Sanderson
The Playboy Firefighter's Proposal	Emily Forbes

HISTORICAL

The Disgraceful Mr Ravenhurst	Louise Allen
The Duke's Cinderella Bride	Carole Mortimer
Impoverished Miss, Convenient Wife	Michelle Styles

MEDICAL™

A Family For His Tiny Twins	Josie Metcalfe
One Night with Her Boss	Alison Roberts
Top-Notch Doc, Outback Bride	Melanie Milburne
A Baby for the Village Doctor	Abigail Gordon

0109 Gen Std LP

MILLS & BOON®
Pure reading pleasure™

FEBRUARY 2009 LARGE PRINT TITLES

ROMANCE

Virgin for the Billionaire's Taking	Penny Jordan
Purchased: His Perfect Wife	Helen Bianchin
The Vásquez Mistress	Sarah Morgan
At the Sheikh's Bidding	Chantelle Shaw
Bride at Briar's Ridge	Margaret Way
Last-Minute Proposal	Jessica Hart
The Single Mum and the Tycoon	Caroline Anderson
Found: His Royal Baby	Raye Morgan

HISTORICAL

Scandalising the Ton	Diane Gaston
Her Cinderella Season	Deb Marlowe
The Warrior's Princess Bride	Meriel Fuller

MEDICAL™

Their Miracle Baby	Caroline Anderson
The Children's Doctor and the Single Mum	Lilian Darcy
The Spanish Doctor's Love-Child	Kate Hardy
Pregnant Nurse, New-Found Family	Lynne Marshall
Her Very Special Boss	Anne Fraser
The GP's Marriage Wish	Judy Campbell

0209 Gen Std HB

MILLS & BOON®
Pure reading pleasure™

MARCH 2009 HARDBACK TITLES

ROMANCE

The Sicilian Boss's Mistress	Penny Jordan
Pregnant with the Billionaire's Baby	Carole Mortimer
The Venadicci Marriage Vengeance	Melanie Milburne
The Ruthless Billionaire's Virgin	Susan Stephens
Capelli's Captive Virgin	Sarah Morgan
Savas' Defiant Mistress	Anne McAllister
The Greek Millionaire's Secret Child	Catherine Spencer
Blackmailed Bride, Innocent Wife	Annie West
Pirate Tycoon, Forbidden Baby	Janette Kenny
Kept by Her Greek Boss	Kathryn Ross
Italian Tycoon, Secret Son	Lucy Gordon
Adopted: Family in a Million	Barbara McMahon
The Billionaire's Baby	Nicola Marsh
Blind-Date Baby	Fiona Harper
Hired: Nanny Bride	Cara Colter
Doorstep Daddy	Shirley Jump
The Baby Doctor's Bride	Jessica Matthews
A Mother For His Twins	Lucy Clark

HISTORICAL

Lord Braybrook's Penniless Bride	Elizabeth Rolls
A Country Miss in Hanover Square	Anne Herries
Chosen for the Marriage Bed	Anne O'Brien

MEDICAL™

The Surgeon She's Been Waiting For	Joanna Neil
The Midwife's New-found Family	Fiona McArthur
The Emergency Doctor Claims His Wife	Margaret McDonagh
The Surgeon's Special Delivery	Fiona Lowe

0209 Gen Std LP

MILLS & BOON®
Pure reading pleasure™

MARCH 2009 LARGE PRINT TITLES

ROMANCE

Ruthlessly Bedded by the Italian Billionaire	Emma Darcy
Mendez's Mistress	Anne Mather
Rafael's Suitable Bride	Cathy Williams
Desert Prince, Defiant Virgin	Kim Lawrence
Wedded in a Whirlwind	Liz Fielding
Blind Date with the Boss	Barbara Hannay
The Tycoon's Christmas Proposal	Jackie Braun
Christmas Wishes, Mistletoe Kisses	Fiona Harper

HISTORICAL

Scandalous Secret, Defiant Bride	Helen Dickson
A Question of Impropriety	Michelle Styles
Conquering Knight, Captive Lady	Anne O'Brien

MEDICAL™

Sheikh Surgeon Claims His Bride	Josie Metcalfe
A Proposal Worth Waiting For	Lilian Darcy
A Doctor, A Nurse: A Little Miracle	Carol Marinelli
Top-Notch Surgeon, Pregnant Nurse	Amy Andrews
A Mother for His Son	Gill Sanderson
The Playboy Doctor's Marriage Proposal	Fiona Lowe